Match Wits with The Hardy Boys®!

Collect the Original
Hardy Boys Mystery Stories
by Franklin W. Dixon

The Tower Treasure
The House on the Cliff
The Secret of the Old Mill
The Missing Chums
Hunting for Hidden Gold
The Shore Road Mystery
The Secret of the Caves
The Mystery of Cabin Island
The Great Airport Mystery
What Happened at Midnight
While the Clock Ticked
Footprints Under the Window
The Mark on the Door
The Hidden Harbor Mystery
The Sinister Signpost
A Figure in Hiding
The Secret Warning
The Twisted Claw
The Disappearing Floor
The Mystery of the Flying Express
The Clue of the Broken Blade
The Flickering Torch Mystery
The Melted Coins
The Short-Wave Mystery
The Secret Panel
The Phantom Freighter
The Secret of Skull Mountain
The Sign of the Crooked Arrow
The Secret of the Lost Tunnel
The Wailing Siren Mystery
The Secret of Wildcat Swamp

The Crisscross Shadow
The Yellow Feather Mystery
The Hooded Hawk Mystery
The Clue in the Embers
The Secret of Pirates' Hill
The Ghost at Skeleton Rock
The Mystery at Devil's Paw
The Mystery of the Chinese Junk
Mystery of the Desert Giant
The Clue of the Screeching Owl
The Viking Symbol Mystery
The Mystery of the Aztec Warrior
The Haunted Fort
The Mystery of the Spiral Bridge
The Secret Agent on Flight 101
Mystery of the Whale Tattoo
The Arctic Patrol Mystery
The Bombay Boomerang
Danger of Vampire Trail
The Masked Monkey
The Shattered Helmet
The Clue of the Hissing Serpent
The Mysterious Caravan
The Witchmaster's Key
The Jungle Pyramid
The Firebird Rocket
The Sting of the Scorpion
Hardy Boys Detective Handbook
The Hardy Boys Back-to-Back
    The Tower Treasure/The House
    on the Cliff

Celebrate 60 Years with the World's Greatest Super Sleuths!

THE WITCHMASTER'S KEY

THERE is no time for explanations when Mr. Hardy tele-
phones Frank and Joe from the West Coast and sends
them flying off to England to help his old friend Professor Rowbotham.

Their stay in East Anglia begins with a weird omen,
as they witness the bizarre funeral of an old witchmaster.
From then on, strange things happen. They are shad-
owed, trapped, sprung upon by a huge black dog, and
smitten by an old crone's curse. Who are their enemies?
The same people who burglarized the professor's witch
museum and robbed him of his life's investment? When
the Hardys learn about the strange disappearance of
Lord Craighead, the plot deepens. Danger lurks every-
where and follows them to Ireland and the Isle of Man.

After surviving a shipwreck in the storm-tossed Irish
Sea, the clue of a frightened white witch leads them
into the torture chamber of a black witches' coven. Frank
and Joe barely escape alive in the final struggle with
their fanatic adversaries, from whom they finally snatch
the telltale Witchmaster's Key!

"My basketball set shot!" Joe whispered.

The Hardy Boys Mystery Stories®

THE WITCHMASTER'S KEY

BY

FRANKLIN W. DIXON

GROSSET & DUNLAP
Publishers • New York
A member of The Putnam & Grosset Group

PRINTED ON RECYCLED PAPER

CONTENTS

THE
WITCHMASTER'S
KEY

CHAPTER I

A Spooky Funeral

As the giant jet hissed toward London, Joe Hardy looked out the window at the flaming sunrise.

"Frank," he said to his brother, "have you made head or tail of this mission?"

"Negative. I couldn't get a solid clue out of Dad. His phone call from California was so hurried. Could it be he's putting us on?"

Joe shrugged. "It wouldn't be like him to send us on a transatlantic wild-goose chase. But it all happened too fast. Not a hint except that we're to help his old friend Professor Chauncey Rowbotham in any way we can."

Airline seats were hard to get at this time of year; so the Hardys had taken the first available flight, even though the professor would be away, lecturing, for another day or two. And only he could brief them properly on their mission!

The boys were used to mysteries. They often

helped their father, Fenton Hardy, the famous private investigator. But they had never been so confused at the start of a case as they were this time.

Frank and Joe had established their reputation by solving the case of *The Tower Treasure*. Their latest, known as *The Mysterious Caravan,* recently took the boys to Morocco. Now, what awaited them in England?

Blond, seventeen-year-old Joe winced, pressing his hand against his cheek.

"That aching wisdom tooth again?" asked Frank, who was dark-haired and a year older.

"Yes. I should have had it pulled before we left J.F.K."

"Hang in there. We'll find you a good English dentist." Trying to distract his brother, Frank went on, "What's your guess about this caper? Forgery, bank robbery, missing person, murder?"

"Maybe old books." Joe tried to smile. "Professor Rowbotham lectures at Cambridge. Perhaps somebody walked off with his Shakespeare collection."

"Could be. Anyhow, we'll know when we get to Griffinmoor in East Anglia."

Joe rubbed his jaw gingerly. "Lucky we don't have to see the professor for two days. That'll give me a chance to get this tooth pulled."

The gentle thud of unlimbering wheels signaled the approach to London airport, and the jet came in for a smooth landing. Passengers yawned and stretched, then filed off the plane.

Joe wrestled their baggage through customs while Frank hired a car at the booth in the terminal.

"We'd better get used to driving on the left side of the road," Frank remarked, as he slid behind the wheel.

"That's for sure," Joe answered. "We don't want to bump heads with some guy coming the other way."

Following the signs, Frank eased the car through roaring London traffic. Near the center of the city they passed a number of vintage automobiles, which bore colorful flags and triangular insignia of shields with crossed arrows and star clusters.

"Who are they?" Frank wondered.

Joe peered back. "London Motor Club. Must be headed for a car show."

Reaching the outskirts of London, Frank stepped on the gas. They sped through the countryside of East Anglia beyond the town of Chelmsford. At Colchester they turned left along the road leading to Ipswich and on north. Just before Norwich, Frank veered east while Joe picked out their route on a map spread across his knees.

"We're in Norfolk County," he said. "Griffinmoor can't be far now."

The car rolled over broad level plains as small

hamlets and big farms slipped by. The boys crossed rickety wooden bridges over slowly meandering streams where windmills stood on the banks, their sails revolving lazily in the breeze. Chickens fluttered away from the car wheels, clucking in fright.

Joe broke the silence. "This is the lowest part of England. Any lower and we'd be under water."

Outside Griffinmoor, Frank eased to a stop to let a funeral procession cross the narrow road.

The mourners were strange-looking people, wearing bedraggled clothes. Six men carried a rough-hewn black coffin on their shoulders, while an unkempt woman followed behind it with a black cat in her arms.

The leader of the procession was a man with a heavy shock of gray hair and a bushy beard. He carried a sword upright in both hands.

The mourners crossed the road in silence. Then they entered the woods on the opposite side and started to chant.

"Abracadabra! Abracadabra! Cast a spell! Cast a spell!"

Frank glanced at his brother. "This is worth a look-see."

"I'll say so," Joe agreed.

Frank ran the car behind a clump of trees and they got out. Creeping through the woods, they followed the funeral procession into an ancient

The mourners crossed the road in silence.

churchyard cemetery high on a hill overlooking Griffinmoor.

Weeds covered the graves, and the headstones were chipped. The nearby church was weather-beaten and deserted.

The Hardys watched from behind a moss-covered tomb while the mourners placed the coffin in an open grave. The leader walked around it three times, pointing at the coffin with his sword. He then struck it three blows with the blade.

The group began to sway from side to side, chanting eerily:

> Power of land and surge of sea,
> Light of moon and might of sun,
> Do as we will and let it be.
> Chant the spell and it is done.

All fell silent as two men lifted the lid off the coffin for the mourners to get a last look at the deceased. Frank and Joe pressed forward for a peek.

They shuddered. The dead man might have been a hundred years old! His wrinkled, wizened face was contorted in a savage scowl!

A low groan broke the silence. The mourners swung around and gazed fiercely at Joe Hardy, whose toothache had caused him to make the sound. Joe tried to look nonchalant, and Frank got ready for action in case the man with the sword decided to use it on them.

The boys were relieved when the mourners went back to burying the dead man. The six pall-bearers quickly shoveled earth on top of the coffin, where it landed with a dull muffled thud.

The people drifted back to the road, and the Hardys returned to their car and resumed their trip.

"I wonder what that get-together meant?" Frank speculated.

"If you ask me," Joe said, "they're making a horror movie."

A few minutes later they were in Griffinmoor, driving down the main street between rows of quaint cottages to the town square. Frank stopped in front of an inn with a signboard showing a soldier in a scarlet coat and steel helmet. They went in.

"Welcome to the Marquis of Granby Inn," the desk clerk greeted them. "What can I do for you?"

"First you can let us have a room," Frank said.

"Righto."

"Second," Joe added as Frank signed the register, "can you tell us about the funeral we passed outside of town?"

The clerk stopped smiling. Nervously he reached for the key to their room and handed it to Frank.

"Number sixteen on the second floor," he said.

"Do enjoy your stay at the Marquis of Granby."

"The funeral," Joe prodded him. "The Boris Karloff characters, who were they?"

The clerk leaned over the desk and said in a low voice, "If you want my advice, you'll forget you ever saw the funeral, because the next one could be yours!"

Thunderstruck by the mysterious warning, the Hardys questioned the clerk further, but he insisted he could tell them nothing more.

"That guy's holding out on us!" Joe said as he and Frank unpacked. "I'd say he's afraid of something."

Frank nodded. "And I'd like to find out what it is."

After washing, they went to the town square and tried to start a conversation with some bowlers on the Griffinmoor green. The men became sullen at the mention of the funeral.

One bowler drew the boys aside. "You're new around here, aren't you?"

"Just over from the U.S.A.," Joe said.

"Then you don't know about old John Pickenbaugh. That was his funeral."

"So?"

"John Pickenbaugh was a witchmaster!"

"Come off it," Joe scoffed. "There aren't any witches."

"You'll know better before you leave East

Anglia," the man retorted, and returned to his game.

The boys inquired in a few Griffinmoor shops. Nobody would talk to them about John Pickenbaugh and his funeral.

"We're getting brush-offs instead of answers," Frank observed.

Finally they came to a run-down tearoom, where a caged parakeet, jars of herbs, and a zodiac chart stood in the window. The name *Mary Ellerbee* was painted on the window ledge. They went in.

Mary Ellerbee was an old woman with a polka-dot bandanna around her head. She offered to read tea leaves for her customers and tell them their fortune. Frank said they'd have tea and cakes but no fortunetelling. They took a corner table.

"Know anything about John Pickenbaugh?" Joe asked before taking a bite of a chocolate cupcake.

"What about old John?" Mary asked suspiciously.

"Was he really a witchmaster?" Frank put in.

"Of course he was! And the mourners at his funeral today were witches from the Griffinmoor coven!"

Frank and Joe exchanged startled glances. Frank lowered his cup of tea. "How do you know that?"

Mary Ellerbee gave a high-pitched cackle. "That's my secret! I'll tell you this, though. You shouldn't be asking about John Pickenbaugh. You should be asking about his successor!"

Joe looked puzzled. "His successor?"

The old woman grinned like a harpy. "Of course. The title is handed down from one witchmaster to another. We've always had a witchmaster in East Anglia."

A black cat leaped into her lap. She stroked its silky fur and whispered something in its ear. The cat yawned, showing long fangs, and peered at the Hardys with green eyes.

Suddenly Mary Ellerbee cackled again, and Joe felt a cold shiver run up his back.

"So!" she cried. "Who do you think is the new witchmaster of East Anglia?"

"Do you know?" Frank asked.

"Maybe I do, and maybe I don't!"

Realizing they would learn nothing more from her, the boys got up. Frank dropped a few British coins on the table.

As they left the tearoom, Mary Ellerbee called out, "Remember East Anglia is witch country of Old England! Strange things happen here!"

As her strident voice died away, they turned down the street toward the Marquis of Granby Inn.

"What an odd character!" Frank said. "But at

least she talked to us. It's lucky we went into her tearoom."

"Not so lucky for me," Joe said. "That chocolate cupcake was a mistake. My jaw feels as though it's blowing up like a basketball!"

"We'd better get you to a dentist, pronto," his brother suggested.

At the inn, Frank found the name of Doctor Vincent Burelli and put through a call. The dentist said it was after hours, but he'd take anybody with a toothache.

The Hardys walked across Griffinmoor just as night was falling. Raindrops pattered down out of a black sky, and the boys sloshed through mud puddles on a side street, looking for the office.

Finally they spotted it and made their way to a door that stood ajar. It bore a nameplate reading: DOCTOR VINCENT BURELLI, DENTAL SURGEON.

Frank rang the bell. No answer. He rang several times. Silence. "Maybe he's treating a patient, Joe. Let's go in."

They found themselves in a tiny waiting room. Through a half-open door on the opposite side they saw the office and the dental chair.

"I don't see any patient or the doctor," Frank said. "We'll have to wait."

They sat down and Frank began to leaf through a magazine on oceanography when footsteps sounded from the direction of the office.

After exchanging perplexed glances, the boys tiptoed across the waiting room and pushed through the door.

Inside they saw an opening trap door beyond the dental chair. A man emerged with his back toward them. He lowered the door and turned around.

The boys gaped. The face was horribly deformed. The eyes bulged. The nose was squashed. A puffy tongue hung limply from a frothing mouth!

CHAPTER II

The Witch Masks

THE horrid-looking creature placed a thumb under his chin and gave a jerk upward. His face came off!

"It's a mask!" Frank cried.

"Only plastic and paint!" Joe marveled.

"Doctor Burelli at your service." The man introduced himself with a low bow.

He was of medium height with short, uncombed brown hair, blue eyes, horn-rimmed glasses, a prominent nose, and an expanding waistline. He smiled easily.

"Quite a start for our visit to Griffinmoor!" Frank mumbled.

"I didn't mean to frighten you," the dentist said seriously. "I'm an amateur actor, and secretary of the Gravesend Players in town. I make masks for our company in my basement workshop. The trap door allows me to work on them between patients. I believe one of you has a toothache. Let me look."

Joe sat down in the dental chair, opened his mouth, and pointed to the sore spot.

"Well," the dentist said after an examination, "You haven't shown much wisdom about that wisdom tooth. The wisest thing would have been to have had it extracted long ago."

He chuckled at his own witticism. Amid a barrage of comic comments, he gave Joe a local anesthetic and waited for it to take effect.

"Who are you fellows?" he inquired. "I notice an American accent."

Frank explained that he and Joe were two Americans who did detective work at home in Bayport. He concealed the fact that they were in Griffinmoor to deal with Professor Rowbotham's mystery. "No sense in gabbing too much," he thought.

Frank was the cautious Hardy. Joe was more likely to leak a secret, but just now Joe couldn't talk.

"So you're detectives," Burelli said. "You must know about masks."

"We use disguises from time to time," Frank admitted.

The dentist clamped his forceps around Joe's tooth, applied leverage, and extracted it.

"No mystery here," he declared. "You see the offender before you. Now you can rinse."

A few minutes later Joe got out of the dental chair, rubbing his jaw.

"Since you're detectives," Burelli went on, "perhaps you'd like to see my collection of masks in the basement."

The boys said they would, and Dr. Burelli lifted the trap door, wedged it open, and descended the ladder. Frank and Joe climbed down after him.

They found themselves in a gloomy room lighted by a single overhead bulb. A long bench held a series of masks of well-known people. They recognized Winston Churchill, General Douglas MacArthur, and Marilyn Monroe.

"A few of my friends," Burelli said airily.

"Those masks wouldn't scare anybody," Joe observed.

The dentist beckoned to them and led the way to another table against a side wall. Four horrid faces with distorted features and misshappen heads glared at them. These masks were as hideous as the one Burelli had worn.

"What an ugly bunch!" Joe exclaimed.

"Worse than the rogues' gallery," Frank added.

The dentist looked pained. "Please! You're talking about the masks I love! Anyway," he said, "I make horror masks for my own amusement."

"Boy, I'd like to have these on Halloween," Joe said. "Nobody could find anything scarier."

Suddenly Burelli became serious and mysterious. "If you think that, look at these!"

He moved to a dark corner that the light of the overhead bulb barely reached. The Hardys could just make out a number of masks that were more sinister than any they'd seen yet.

A man's mask peered at them through slitted eyes, the corners of the mouth turned up in a malevolent smirk. A woman's face was wild-eyed, the nostrils flaring, the mouth open as if to bite.

Frank and Joe shivered in spite of their long experience with criminals. They had never come across faces that exuded evil, as these masks did.

"I thought you'd be impressed," Burelli stated.

"What are they?" Frank wondered.

"Witch masks!"

Joe shook his head as if he were coming out of a trance. "What are witch masks?"

"Faces copied from woodcuts and pictures of witches in old books," Burelli explained. "I make drawings of the witches and then design the masks. I read the old records of witch trials to get in the mood before I start work on a witch mask."

"They're enough to give anyone the willies," Joe said.

"Well," the doctor answered, "you two are the only ones who have gotten the willies, if I may use your expression, because you're the only ones who have seen my witch masks."

"Why the secrecy?" Joe wanted to know.

"You'll find out soon enough if you stay in Griffinmoor. Now then, we'd better go upstairs.

Another patient may be waiting. I hope you'll keep this under your hat. I don't want word of what I'm doing to get around."

The Hardys assured him they'd keep his secret. Burelli revealed that he was hoping for a one-man exhibit of his masks in London.

"That show'll scare the public," Frank predicted.

"Thanks for the compliment," Burelli said.

They climbed back up the ladder and the dentist lowered the trap door into place. A faint smell hung in the atmosphere, reminding Joe of the Bayport riding stables.

"Don't tell me you have a horse in the waiting room," he quipped.

"Nothing as spectacular as that," Burelli said with a grin.

"Quit the bloody jokes," a voice called out. "I've been waiting for ages!"

"That's Nip Hadley," Burelli informed the Hardys. "He's the groom of the Craighead estate. Cracked a tooth this afternoon, playing soccer. He made an appointment with me just after you called."

The dentist led the way into the waiting room. Nip Hadley was Joe's age and height, but more stocky in his build and rough in his demeanor. His husky shoulders showed that he had the strength to handle a horse.

Burelli introduced them. Joe offered his hand

but the groom refused. He glared at the Hardys.

"I heard about you Yanks. You been asking questions about old John Pickenbaugh. Pretty nosy, ain't you?"

"We just stumbled on the funeral," Frank protested.

"Sure," Nip jeered. "You might get a bang on the snoot if you keep pushing it in where it ain't wanted. And I'm the one who'll do the banging!"

The boy's challenge was too much for Joe to take. He moved forward with his fists up, ready to swing at Nip.

Burelli quickly stepped between them. "You fellows seem anxious to keep me in business. But I'm not looking for any more right now. There's been enough dental damage for one day." He and Nip went into the office, while the Hardys walked into the street and headed back toward the inn.

"Nip Hadley seems like a tough customer," Joe remarked. "He's about as friendly as a bear with a sore head."

"He sure wouldn't win any popularity contest," Frank agreed. "But your remarks didn't help. Maybe you wouldn't feel friendly if you had a cracked tooth and somebody said you smelled like a horse."

"I guess you're right," Joe confessed. "I'll apologize if we meet Nip again."

"Chances are, in this little town you will," Frank replied.

"You know, there's something eerie about this place," Joe went on. "No one wants to talk about John Pickenbaugh or the witch business; and all we get are cryptic warnings about finding out about it if we stay in Griffinmoor long enough."

Frank nodded thoughtfully. "I didn't expect anything like this. Everyone is a little strange. Did you ever hear of a dentist whose hobby is making witch masks?"

Joe laughed. "No, but why not? I like Dr. Burelli. He seems to be a good dentist and a jolly good fellow, too. Maybe all the jaws he sees day after day inspire him to make those crazy masks."

The rain began to fall harder. As the Hardys turned a corner, they stepped into a gooey mud puddle and had to scramble out.

"My shoes are a mess!" Joe complained.

"Mine, too."

They hastened back to the inn and went to bed. They were sleeping soundly when they became dimly aware of a commotion going on downstairs.

Joe opened one eye and looked at his watch. "Six o'clock!" He groaned. "You'd think they'd hold their karate exercises later in the day!"

"Something must be up," Frank said.

Heavy feet pounded up the stairs. A fist banged loudly on their door. Frank jumped out of bed and opened it. Joe joined him.

A tall police constable stood there.

"Are you Frank and Joe Hardy?" he asked.

"Yes, we are. What's the matter?" Frank inquired.

The constable glowered at them. "John Pickenbaugh's grave was robbed during the night! I'd like to ask you a few questions. Anything you say may be taken down and used in evidence against you!"

CHAPTER III

Graveyard Surprise!

"WHAT? You mean we're being arrested for grave robbery?" Joe exploded.

"Cool it, Joe," Frank urged his brother. "We haven't been charged with any crime."

"Not yet," the constable explained. "But you'll have to come with me for questioning."

At headquarters the constable grilled them about their stay in Griffinmoor.

"How did your shoes get muddy?" he asked.

"We blundered into a mud puddle last night," Frank said.

"Perhaps you were digging up the body of John Pickenbaugh," the constable contended.

Joe got hot under the collar. "What would we want with a corpse? We didn't even know the guy!"

"That's what you say," the constable noted.

Suddenly he fired a question at them. "What do you know about witchcraft?"

Frank coolly fielded the question. "Not a thing, constable. America had witch trials in Salem. But this was long before our time."

"We have an alibi," Joe said. "We weren't there."

The constable cleared his throat. "Where were you last night at ten o'clock?"

"That's easy," Frank told him. "In bed at the Marquis of Granby Inn. Why don't you check with the desk clerk?"

The constable picked up the phone and put a call through. After a brief conversation, he hung up.

"Okay," he said. "Your alibi checks out. The manager tells me you came in long before that and did not leave again."

"Does that mean we can go?" Frank asked.

"Not quite. I'll need a character reference. Will anyone in Griffinmoor vouch for you?"

Frank scratched his head. "I guess the only one is Professor Chauncey Rowbotham."

"Yeah," Joe put in. "He knows who we are."

The constable called the professor, who just had arrived at his home. Rowbotham said he would be right over. While they waited, Frank and Joe talked to the men at headquarters about British methods of crime fighting. They gathered a few tips to add to their criminology files in Bayport.

Professor Rowbotham bustled in. He was slight, with a goatee and flowing white hair. He carried a cane, which he waved around so carelessly that he nearly hit the constable. He stammered slightly as he talked.

After admitting he had never met the Hardys, he was challenged about how he could vouch for them.

"But—ah—ah, I know the father of these young men," he said. "The sons of Fenton Hardy are sure to be all right."

"Professor," the constable said, "your word is good enough for me." He turned to Frank and Joe. "Okay, you're free to go."

Rowbotham had a European compact car outside. While they drove, he explained the mystery that had brought them to East Anglia.

"Ah—ah, well, you see, the fact is, I'm curator of the Griffinmoor Witch Museum. It's my life's work. All my money is tied up in it."

Joe nudged Frank. Griffinmoor seemed to be crowded with witches.

"So you want us to investigate the ladies who ride broomsticks?" Joe suggested.

"No—er—no, nothing like that. The problem is that the museum has been robbed. Burglarized! Cleaned out! I hope you fellows can find out who did it, because the police don't seem to make any headway."

They drove up to a large building not far from

the cemetery where they had spied on the weird Pickenbaugh funeral. It was four stories high with a lot of corners and bay windows. The slate roof tilted at a steep angle that made it appear to be toppling over.

Professor Rowbotham escorted them through a few rooms of the Witchcraft Museum. All were stripped completely.

"Not even a stick of furniture left," Frank muttered.

"Quite—that is—I would have to say you are quite right. Nothing is left. Everything is gone. The basement is here. I had a big collection of occult items down there. The rooms were locked. Now they are empty!"

"Why would the thieves take everything?" Joe wondered. "Why didn't they concentrate on valuable objects?"

Frank pinched his lower lip. "They may have been after something specific," he theorized. "Maybe they took everything so nobody could tell which piece they wanted."

Rowbotham was impressed by the theory. "Very likely, very likely. But I cannot imagine what it could be. I wrote to your father because I was so stunned. I thought he might solve the mystery."

"Dad was delayed by an important case in California," Frank said. "He sent us instead."

"I see—I see your point. I understand he

trained you to be detectives. But ah—ah—the question is, will you take the case?"

"Of course we will, professor," Joe assured him. "That's what we're here for."

"First of all," Frank said, "is there any tie-in between the burglary at the Witch Museum and the robbery of John Pickenbaugh's grave?"

Professor Rowbotham said he doubted it. "Pickenbaugh was still alive when the theft took place," he pointed out.

"Have there been any other burglaries around here?" Frank asked.

"Ah—ah—yes. There've been some at Eagleton Green. That is the artisan village next to Griffinmoor."

"Artisan village?" Frank queried.

"A village of workmen who make things like clocks, guns, and jewelry. They have suffered from thefts lately, also arson."

"Theft and arson!" Joe exclaimed. "Sounds like a gang operating in East Anglia!"

"But—ah—ah, although I'm not a detective," Rowbotham said, "I must tell you these were small crimes. More like harassment."

"Any suspects?" Frank persisted.

"A young man, a groom, I believe, from the Craighead estate."

"Nip Hadley?" Joe blurted out.

"Just so. He was caught near the Eagleton

Green Saddle Shop just after a fire bomb went off."

"We've met him," Joe said. "He might just be mean enough to do something like that."

"Don't jump to conclusions," Frank advised. "Let's talk to Nip about this." He turned to Rowbotham. "What kind of objects are we talking about? I'd like to know a witch collection when I see one."

The professor produced a thick catalog. Frank and Joe studied the listings.

"Wow!" Joe exclaimed. "Cauldrons, robes, wands, bells, daggers, dolls with pins in them—the works!"

"Also," Frank observed, "stuffed animals, astrology charts, poison potions, and the good old skull and crossbones."

Rowbotham cleared his throat. "Notice the instruments of torture. They are my particular hobby. Pincers, thumbscrews, headsman's ax, etcetera."

Frank closed the catalog and handed it back. "With so many items involved," he said, "we'll have to go over this museum with a fine-toothed comb."

"But ah—ah—, the police have already done so," Rowbotham declared. "They even found a clue, and took it to headquarters."

"Then we'd better mosey on down there and take a look at it," Joe said.

"We'll be back later," Frank promised.

"You'll stay with me," the professor said, "in my house behind the museum. I'll have your things brought over from the inn."

"Sure thing, professor. Thanks. Meanwhile we'll return our car. I doubt that we'll need it."

At headquarters they spoke to an officious sergeant named Joseph Rankin. When they asked about the clue from the Witch Museum, Rankin at first evaded the issue.

"Why should I say anything to you about the clue?" he growled.

"Because Professor Rowbotham hired us to investigate this case for him," Frank said in a conciliatory tone. Quickly he filled the sergeant in.

"Well," Rankin said, "in that case you might as well see what we found."

He opened a drawer and produced a long purple-and-white feather, which he placed on the desk. "This was on the floor beside the door of the museum."

"Any theory about it?" Frank queried.

"We know feathers were used to make witches' brew. The thieves must have dropped it when they were moving the stuff out the door."

"Then it was part of Professor Rowbotham's collection?"

"He claims not. But why would anyone bring a feather along on a burglary job?"

"Thanks, sergeant," Joe said.

"We appreciate it," Frank added.

As the boys started for Rowbotham's home, Joe said, "I think that's an eagle feather."

"Not exactly an eagle," Frank disagreed, "but a close relative. I'm not sure. What bugs me, though, is that the professor claims it's not his."

Joe had an inspiration. "What say we make a detour around by the cemetery and take a gander at Pickenbaugh's grave?"

"Good idea. Maybe the ghouls left a clue."

They tramped through the woods to the spot where they had seen the weird mourners. The police were there, examining the empty coffin that had held the corpse of the witchmaster.

A few questions elicited the information that no clue to the desecration had been found.

Frank and Joe went up to one of the officers. "Found anything yet?" Frank asked.

The tall, thin man shook his head. Then he squinted. "What's it to you?"

"We were accused of pulling this little job this morning," Joe answered angrily. "So we're interested."

"Oh, you are the American fellows who are visiting here," the officer said with a grin of recognition. "They tried to pin it on you but it didn't stick. Well, it looks like a burglary to me. The lining of the coffin was ripped as if the villains were looking for something hidden in there."

"But why would they take the corpse, then?" Joe asked.

The officer shrugged. "Who knows?"

"Let's look around the cemetery," Frank suggested. "Maybe we'll find something the cops overlooked."

They walked between headstones until they came to a freshly dug grave. Frank advanced to the edge of the hole and peered into it. Joe moved up beside him.

A sudden slithering noise made them whirl around. Two hooded figures leaped on them from behind a clump of bushes. Two clubs descended in a swinging arc. *Zap!* Everything went black!

Frank and Joe tumbled headfirst into the open grave and lay still!

CHAPTER IV

A Night Search

FRANK came to and sat up, rubbing the back of his head. Joe stirred beside him.

Footsteps sounded nearby, and in moments several people formed a ring around the grave and gazed down at the two boys.

"Young men," said a clergyman, "what are you doing in this grave? We are about to hold a funeral!"

"Pretty embarrassing," Frank muttered. He said aloud, "We fell in accidentally. Sorry about that."

Some of the men bent down and helped the Hardys out. Nip Hadley was one of them. The mourners frowned as Frank and Joe stepped hastily past the coffin and made for the woods. Nip followed them.

Joe turned around. "Say, Nip, I want to apologize for being rude at the dentist's the other day. I didn't mean it."

"That's all right, I wasn't my usual lovey self either. That tooth hurt a lot!" Nip grinned, then went on, "What happened? I don't go for that accident stuff."

"A couple of goons conked us," Frank said. "I didn't see who they were. Did you, Joe?"

"Negative. But you got to the scene of the crime awfully quick, Nip. How come?"

The groom looked hurt. "I followed the funeral procession, just like you guys did with John Pickenbaugh. Bushwhacking ain't my style."

"Okay, if you say so, Nip," Frank said.

The groom changed the subject. "Know what's happening at headquarters? You two are accused of being witches!"

Frank and Joe halted in their tracks. "Witches!" Joe exploded. "Who says that?"

"Old Mary Ellerbee. They say she's a witch herself and was a member of old John Pickenbaugh's coven. Anyhow, she was at his funeral."

Something clicked in Joe's mind. "The old woman carrying the black cat! I didn't recognize her at the tearoom because of the bandanna she was wearing."

"Come on, Joe!" Frank said. "We'd better get over there. Thanks for the tip, Nip."

They found Mary Ellerbee at the police station. She was clutching an ancient book in her hands.

"Apprehend them!" she cried as they entered.

"What's the charge?" Frank inquired.

"Malicious mischief!"

"Where's the proof?" Joe challenged.

"Right here in this book. It says Melinda Hardy Smith was a Salem witch sentenced to be drowned. She was your ancestor. So you're both warlocks. You're up to mischief in Griffinmoor! If you didn't rob John's grave, you ordered it done!"

The Hardys knew that a warlock was a male witch.

"There's one big hole in your theory," Frank said mildly. "Our ancestors weren't in America at the time of the Salem witch trials. So Melinda Hardy Smith has nothing to do with us."

"That settles it," a policeman said.

Furiously Mary Ellerbee stalked out, shouting strident threats as she went.

"She sure has it in for us," Joe said. "I wonder why?"

"Your guess is as good as mine, Joe."

They decided to let their parents know what was happening to them in England. At a telegraph office, they sent a cable to Bayport, explaining that they were on the Rowbotham case but had made little headway.

"It's nice to be in touch with home," Joe stated. "Here everyone is against us."

"Except Professor Rowbotham and Dr. Burelli," Frank said. "You know something? I wish Chet and Phil were here with us."

Chet Morton and Phil Cohen, their Bayport pals, were on a bicycle tour of Ireland. They often helped the Hardys solve cases.

At Rowbotham's home, the Hardys walked up along the semicircular drive to the house, where they found that the professor had installed them in a bedroom on the ground floor opposite the Witch Museum. They questioned him about the purple-and-white feather at the police station.

"It was definitely—ah—not in my collection," he said emphatically. "A strange feather, incidentally. I would almost suspect it came from the mythical beast of Griffinmoor—the griffin, half eagle and half lion. Here, let me show you the Griffinmoor emblem."

He led them into his study and pointed to a plaque on the wall. It showed a fierce eagle with a lion's head, flying off into the sky while bearing a knight in armor in its talons.

The legend at the bottom read: "Norman invaders were repulsed here by the eagle with gigantic talons." Below that was the motto: *Avoir la Serre Bonne.*

"The motto is in French," the professor explained. "It means, 'to have a strong grip.' I imagine you realize the significance of such a motto."

"When Griffinmoor grabs you," Frank suggested, "it never lets go."

"Ah—ah—that interpretation will do very well. Yes."

Joe felt restless. "But what do *we* do is what I want to know. This confab isn't doing anything to solve the mystery."

Frank looked at Rowbotham. "Professor, I think Joe and I should search your museum. The police may have missed something."

"As you wish," Rowbotham conceded, and gave him the key.

They reached the tall, dark building just as dusk was falling. It had an air of sinister foreboding about it.

Frank unlocked the heavy door. They went in and Joe snapped on the master light for the building.

Wham! A gust of wind caught the door and slammed it shut behind them. The sound echoed through the cavernous Witch Museum.

"Sounds like ghosts upstairs," Frank said.

"Witches would be more like it," Joe noted. "This place gives me the creeps."

"Me too. It's spooky."

Hurrying up three flights of stairs, they entered the attic, a large room supported by rough crossbeams covered with dust and cobwebs. The walls slanted inward, and the Hardys could see the steep slate roof through a tiny window.

A pitch-black raven perched on the topmost pinnacle. As they watched, it emitted a loud, hoarse croak and flew off in the direction of the churchyard, which was visible in the distance.

The rising wind shook the top of the Witch Museum. Rain lashed the tiles outside. A bolt of lightning cut through the sky. Thunder boomed overhead.

Ignoring the storm, the Hardys inspected the attic thoroughly.

"See anything?" Joe asked.

"Couple of spiders. That's about it."

They went down a flight of squeaky stairs to the third floor. A sign on the door read: WITCHES' BREW.

Inside they found rows of shelves on the walls, reaching from the floor to the ceiling. They were labeled with the names of witch poisons, ointments, recipes, and herbs. But the shelves were bare.

"Boy, Professor Rowbotham sure kept a lot of powerful stuff in here," Frank commented. "Hemlock, belladonna, aconite——"

"Also henbane," Joe added.

The Hardys knew these were deadly poisons. Frank gave Joe a worried look.

"Remember when I asked you on the plane what the East Anglia case might involve? Maybe it's poison!"

Joe shuddered. "There must be a lot of this stuff floating around Griffinmoor, Frank. And the thieves might not know what it is!"

There was a rustling movement near the door. Something hurtled at them, aimed straight for Joe's head!

Before he could move, the projectile veered off onto a high rafter.

"A bat!" Frank chuckled.

"Very funny," Joe groused.

Another set of rickety stairs brought them to the second floor of the Witch Museum. Here the sign read: EFFIGY ROOM.

Frank scrutinized the place. "This is where the witches lived. Statues of them, anyway. I remember the pictures in Professor Rowbotham's catalog. They showed witches in robes and Halloween hats, carrying candles. One held a crystal ball in the palm of her hand."

"Don't forget the witchmaster, Frank. He stood over here with a sword in his hands, just like the guy we saw leading the funeral procession to John Pickenbaugh's grave."

The Hardys descended to the main floor.

"We went through these rooms with Professor Rowbotham," Joe said. "No need for a repeat performance."

Frank nodded. A grandfather clock tolled loudly from a dark passageway. Boards creaked overhead.

"Joe!" Frank exclaimed, "I hear footsteps!"

"Probably a cat, Frank. A black cat, witch style.

Come on. We've only got the basement and the sub-basement. Let's get this over with!"

The basement walls were faced with brick. This was where Professor Rowbotham had kept his instruments of torture. Chains hung on the walls, but everything else was gone.

"Not my idea of a home away from home," Joe said.

"Frankenstein's castle," Frank suggested, "or Dracula's."

The boys sounded the brick walls and the floor as they made their round of the basement. Since nothing suspicious caught their attention, they turned to a small wooden door on rusty hinges. Frank forced the bolt back. The hinges grated harshly as he drew it open.

A narrow stairway met their eyes. It fell deeply into total darkness.

"Obviously the sub-basement is not connected to the master switch. Maybe there's a separate one downstairs," Frank said.

He descended the staircase, guiding himself with a flashlight he had brought along.

"There's the switch," he said, flicking on a dim bulb and returning the flashlight to his pocket.

They found themselves in a musty dark room with a ceiling so low they could touch it by raising a hand. The flagstones that made up the floor were interspersed with ancient tombstones.

"If rheumatism is your bag," Joe quipped, "this is the place to get it."

"I hope we can get a clue to the burglary," Frank said. "I'll start on the opposite side. You begin here. We can compare notes after scouting around."

"Okay," Joe said.

Frank started across the stone floor. Joe walked along the wall next to the staircase. The clammy chill of the place began to seep into their bones.

Joe shivered. "It's like being buried alive!"

"Pick your gravestone," Frank joked, then added seriously, "Wait a minute! I see something! Joe, look at this!"

Frank had hardly spoken when the light went out. The Hardys were plunged into utter darkness!

CHAPTER V

The Runaway Horse

FRANK pulled out his flashlight, snapped it on, and played the beam around the room.

"Someone fiddled with the fuse box," Joe muttered. "Or a fuse blew by itself."

"Let's find out. It's probably in the basement."

The boys ascended the staircase. The basement was just as dark. Frank found the fuse box and lifted the cover.

The master fuse was turned down!

"That explains it," Joe said. "Somebody put the whammy on the whole lighting system."

"Whoever did it," Frank said, "doesn't want us around. Must be afraid we'll find a clue." Joe pushed the master fuse back in place, and the museum lighted up again.

Quickly the Hardys searched the entire building, but found nobody.

"Whoever pulled that trick got away," Joe said, "via the front door. We left it unlocked."

"We won't make that mistake again," Frank said, and he turned the key. Then they hurried down to the sub-basement to see what Frank had discovered.

"Look here," he said, using his flashlight for extra illumination. He pointed to a hole in the wall. It seemed to have been gouged out with some kind of tool, leaving a residue of fine dust.

Joe rubbed some between his fingers. "Frank, this is dry, not damp like the rest of the room."

"That means the hole was dug out recently!"

"Righto. You know, I believe something might have been hidden here! This could be the clue that breaks the case!" Joe said, excited.

"We'll make a cast of the hole even though it is very rough," Frank said, "and try to figure out what it was! Maybe Nip Hadley can get us the stuff we need for the job."

"Good idea. We can kill two birds with one stone by talking to Nip about his troubles."

They went upstairs, turned out the lights, and left the building. The next day they walked past Eagleton Green on their way to the sprawling Craighead estate, stopping momentarily to look into the windows to see the artisans at work.

Finally the turrets of Craighead Castle loomed ahead. They towered over medieval battlements, with embrasures for shooting arrows at enemies beyond the drawbridge.

Before they reached the castle, they noticed the stables and corral in a field beyond. Nip, wearing a jaunty striped cap, was exercising a lively black horse.

Holding the reins in one hand, he pulled the animal up on its hind legs. Then he let it have its head in a canter. Finally he spurred into a gallop, took his mount over a couple of hedges, wheeled in a wide arc, and hurtled toward the Hardys. He pulled to a stop and jumped to the ground beside them.

"Nice ride, Nip," Frank said.

"Better than Buffalo Bill," Joe added.

Nip grinned. "Let me introduce Midnight, a skittish horse and a smart one."

"Smart?" Joe wondered.

Nip slapped the animal's neck. "He knows how to get the corral gate open. Sometimes he does a disappearing act and we have to chase after him. What brings you to Griffinmoor?"

Joe explained the clue at the Witch Museum and asked Nip if he could collect the ingredients for a cast.

"What do you need?" the groom asked.

"Two half-gallon cans, one containing plaster of Paris, the other empty. A can of clear plastic spray, and a wooden stick for stirring."

"Sure, I can get all that," Nip said. He offered to show them the grounds. "First, though, I'll have to dispose of Midnight."

He led the black horse to a corral. After opening the gate, he slapped the animal on the rump, urging it to amble in, then closed the gate.

He escorted the Hardys past the main hall of Craighead Castle and along a winding path to the stables.

"Those are my quarters," Nip said, pointing to a window under the eaves above the stables.

"Do you like being a groom?" Frank inquired.

"Rather! I was born in East Anglia. Went to school in Griffinmoor. Raised with horses. So, I was lucky to be appointed groom when I asked Mr. Craighead for a job."

The three strolled up a small hill overlooking the tilled farmland. Beyond lay an orchard. On the other side of the hill stood a stone wall.

"This wall," Nip said, "divides the land belonging to the Craighead estate from that of Eagleton Green. Some awfully strange things are going on over there."

"Like what?" Frank asked.

Nip cocked his head to one side and squinted at them as if making up his mind.

"I suppose I can trust you blokes," he said. "You know those robberies and fires in the artisan shops? Well, I think it's sabotage!"

Frank looked incredulous. "You mean some-

Nip came hurtling toward the Hardys.

body's trying to put the craftsmen out of business?"

Nip shrugged. "Looks that way."

"But why?"

"I haven't any idea."

The three boys walked along a path leading to the rear of Craighead Castle. The sheer wall towered above them. Nip said the main windows belonged to the kitchen and dining room.

"What's up there?" Joe asked, pointing to a tiny window that glinted in the sun high up in one turret.

"Don't really know," Nip confessed, whereupon Frank brought the conversation back to the Eagleton Green mystery.

He asked about the charge that Nip had firebombed the saddle shop. The boy was about to answer when they turned a corner of the castle and saw a man approaching them. He wore a riding outfit and held a whip in one hand.

Nip introduced him to the Hardys as Milton Craighead, owner of the Craighead estate.

Milton was about thirty years old. He was stiff and formal, barely shaking hands with Frank and Joe as if it went against the grain. While saying a few words to them, he cracked his whip against his boot.

All at once loud cries interrupted him. A gardener was shouting, "Midnight is loose! Catch him! Catch him!"

"He escaped from the corral again!" Nip exclaimed.

Milton scowled. "How could that possibly have happened? Maybe we've had visitors who left the gate open!"

"He means Frank and me," Joe thought. "Not a very friendly fellow."

Milton and Nip raced to the stables and leaped on horses. They set out in pursuit of the runaway, which was galloping around the pasture. Frank and Joe followed on foot. There was a wild chase in which Midnight dodged several times.

Frank stood still for a moment in the middle of the pasture, shielding his eyes as he watched the black horse.

Suddenly he heard the thunder of hoofbeats in his ears. Turning sideways, he saw Milton's mount coming at him full tilt!

CHAPTER VI

The Missing Marquis

Nip galloped up, grabbed the bridle of Milton's mount, and forced it to swing wide, brushing Frank and knocking him over. Both horses halted.

Milton Craighead mopped his brow with a handkerchief. "I lost control," he said in a shaky voice. "I hope you're not hurt."

Frank scrambled to his feet. "Only a few bruises," he reported.

"That's fortunate." Craighead seemed relieved. "Nip, let's get after Midnight."

The pursuers cornered the runaway in an angle of the stone wall. Nip threw a rope over its neck and led it back to the corral. While Milton made sure the gate was fastened, Frank and Joe had a quick conversation with Nip Hadley.

"Thanks for the assist," Frank said.

Joe stressed the point. "You probably saved Frank's life, Nip. We'll do anything we can to help you. Just tell us what you know about the fire-bombing in Eagleton Green."

"I can't talk now," Nip replied uneasily. "I'll see you later and bring those things you need."

Milton finished with the gate and walked toward them. "It's securely fastened now," he said. "If that horse escapes again, I'll want to know the reason why. Nip, keep an eye on all strangers."

Frank and Joe inferred that this was an invitation for them to leave the Craighead estate. They went back to the professor's, where they discussed their visit.

Why was Milton Craighead hostile toward them? Had he really lost control of his mount? Or was he trying to run Frank down?

The Hardys wondered. The case was becoming more and more mysterious.

Nip rode up later with the ingredients for the plaster cast in his saddle bags. Saying he couldn't wait because Craighead wanted him to break in a new horse, he emptied the bags quickly and rode off.

Frank and Joe went to the Witch Museum, made their way to the sub-basement with a container of water and got ready to make a cast of the hollowed-out part of the wall. They had often lifted impressions of footprints and tire tracks. In fact, they had devised the Hardy Plaster-Cast Kit, made up of the items they had asked Nip to bring.

Joe covered the break in the wall with plastic

spray to firm up the dust and broken particles. He poured some water into the plaster of Paris, and stirred the paste to the proper consistency.

Then he pressed some into the depression with the stick. When it became firm enough, Frank inserted small bits of wood to fortify the cast as it solidified. Then he added the remaining plaster.

When it had dried sufficiently, Frank pried out the cast with his pocketknife and laid it on the floor. They now had an impression of the object that had been concealed in the wall. It seemed to be a straight cylindrical object about eight inches long and half an inch wide.

"Could have been an iron bar," Frank said. "But there's a loop at one end and a wedge at the other. Professor Rowbotham might be able to identify it."

They took the plaster cast to the house. Rowbotham inspected it carefully.

"Ah—ah, this appears to be the impression of a key. A very old, very ornate, very large key."

"A key to what?" Joe asked.

"As to that, I cannot say. But such keys were used in English castles long ago."

"Craighead Castle!" Frank blurted. "It may open a door in Craighead Castle!"

"Possibly," Rowbotham agreed. "However, you cannot get in there. Milton Craighead does not like strangers."

"We know," Joe said with a dry chuckle.

"Ah—ah, besides, a mystery hangs over the place."

"What mystery, Professor?" Joe asked.

"The mystery of the missing marquis!"

Frank and Joe each felt tingles of excitement. Eagerly they urged Rowbotham to go on.

The professor said that the missing marquis, Lord Craighead, had been a distinguished soldier.

"Five years ago he announced his intention of visiting his old mates in Dublin. His servants helped him pack. His son, Milton, bade him farewell and he rode away in his car."

Rowbotham paused for breath. The Hardys sat motionless, waiting for him to continue.

"The marquis hasn't been seen since!"

"Not a sign of him?" Joe asked.

"In five years?" Frank exclaimed.

"Just so," the professor assured them.

A shuffling sound outside the door broke into their thoughts. Frank put his finger to his lips. Getting up, he tiptoed across the room, silently turned the knob, and jerked the door open.

A tall, stooped man with white hair stood outside. He was Sears, Rowbotham's butler.

"Were you listening at the door?" Frank demanded.

"Not at all, sir. I was bringing in the tea." He lifted a large pot from a tea wagon and placed it on the table.

Joe, suspicious, questioned Sears closely. "Did

you let the thieves into the Witch Museum?"

"No sir. The robbery took place on my night off."

"That's why I went out to dinner with an old friend," Rowbotham confirmed.

After Sears had left, Frank said, "He could have doubled back and met a gang of confederates."

"Impossible!" the professor said forcefully. "I trust Sears implicitly."

They broke up after tea and the Hardys devised a new strategy. Frank had the first idea.

"We must have a key made from our plaster cast."

"Let's try Eagleton Green," Joe suggested. "There must be a locksmith among the artisans."

In the village, they walked along the main street and stopped at a gunsmith's for information.

He told them to go to the shop of Lance McKnight, the locksmith.

McKnight was a rough-looking character with a heavy growth of beard. His shop was cluttered and dusty. Swords, daggers, and other weapons hung on the walls and a pile of keys lay on the counter.

McKnight claimed he could make keys from plaster casts. But when the boys produced theirs, his demeanor changed. He became evasive. "That's a tough job," he grumbled.

"You do tough jobs, don't you?" Frank asked.

"Sure. But not that tough. The plaster isn't right."

"It's the best East Anglia plaster."

"Well, the cast is too big."

"Why is it too big?" Joe pressured him.

The keymaker became surly. "Because I say it is. I don't want the job."

They asked if he knew someone else who could do the job.

"Not here," McKnight replied. "Possibly in London. See Matthew Hopkins at the East Anglia Inn. He's a wealthy, well-informed man who knows just about everyone in the city."

As they walked back through Eagleton Green, Frank said, "McKnight wasn't very friendly."

"He sure changed his tune when he saw our plaster cast. I can't figure out why."

At the East Anglia Inn, Matthew Hopkins was having dinner. His greeting was friendly, and he listened with interest to the story of how they had made their cast.

"Yes," he said, fingering the watch chain across his vest. "I know just the place in London where you can have a key made. It's in Soho Square. Here, let me write the address on my card."

Joe took the card, and the boys thanked him.

"Don't mention it," Hopkins replied in a hearty tone. "I'm always glad to be of any service to our American friends." He went back to his dinner.

Frank and Joe returned to the lobby. They saw that one side of the card bore the printed legend: *Matthew Hopkins, Real Estate, Berkeley Square, London.* On the other side, Hopkins had written: *"Marshall Street, Soho, opposite the Medmenham Book Store."*

"We'll go tomorrow," Frank said.

They took the short route across a wide meadow. Night had fallen, and the sky was cloudy. Leaves rustled as trees bent in the wind.

The Hardys were in the middle of the field when they heard a long drawn-out howl that drew rapidly nearer. The howl changed to a ferocious snarl.

An immense black dog with snapping fangs hurled itself at Joe. The younger Hardy hit the turf. The dog sailed over him, landed on the ground, and vanished into the darkness.

"Let's get out of here, fast!" Joe grated as he got up.

Frank gulped. "I'd just as soon not have another brush with the Hound of the Baskervilles! I guess we're lucky that he's obviously trained to frighten only and not to attack!"

They hastened out of the meadow and back to Rowbotham's house, where they recounted their adventures in Eagleton Green. When they got to the incident of the dog in the meadow, the professor gasped.

"What's the matter?" Joe asked. "Do you by any chance know who owns the dog?"

"He didn't bite Joe," Frank added. "On the other hand. I doubt that he tried to jump us without being told."

The professor nodded. His stammer became more pronounced. "Ah—ah, your tale is—ah— what I might term incredible. A witch dog, the black hound of Norfolk, used to be seen in this part of East Anglia!"

CHAPTER VII

Curious Yanks

"THE Black Hound of Norfolk prowled by night," Rowbotham explained. "Anybody he bit turned into a witch!"

Joe shuddered. "Looks as if I had a closer call than we thought. If I hadn't ducked, I might be a witch right now!"

Rowbotham smiled wryly. "However," he went on, "there is genuine history about the witchcraft of East Anglia. And I must tell you that the name Matthew Hopkins is ominous."

Frank frowned and protested that he hadn't noticed anything ominous about the real-estate man from London. Joe agreed.

"Ah—ah, the point is that there was a man named Matthew Hopkins in the seventeenth century, who called himself the Witch-finder of East Anglia. He investigated those who were suspected of witchcraft. He used what you Americans call the 'third degree' to force confessions. And he executed many. You came through Chelmsford on the way to Griffinmoor?"

"Yes," Frank answered.

"Exactly. Well, in the year 1645 Matthew Hopkins hanged nineteen witches in one day at Chelmsford. But that's not all. When the Witchfinder General died, it came to light that he was a witch himself!"

"Wow!" Joe exclaimed. "The guy covered himself by pretending he hated witches!"

Rowbotham chuckled and said that the people of East Anglia were shocked when they learned Hopkins was a witch.

The Hardys noted that the Matthew Hopkins they were dealing with didn't look like a witch.

Rowbotham held up a hand. "Ah—ah, that's what they thought of the Witchfinder General in Cromwell's time. You must admit there's a strange coincidence in the two men having the same name. I would advise you to be careful in dealing with any man called Matthew Hopkins."

They were preparing for bed when they heard a scratching sound on the window pane. It was Nip Hadley, who motioned to them to let him in. When Frank threw the window up, Nip slipped over the sill into the room.

Hurriedly he told them of more sabotage at

the Eagleton Green artisan village. He was afraid he might be accused of setting more fires.

"And I didn't even set the one at the saddle shop," he said.

"Maybe you were framed," Joe said.

Nip groaned. "Framed! That's it! Will you blokes help me?"

Frank and Joe said they would do what they could to prove his innocence. A sudden thought struck Joe. "Nip, are there any other witch collections around here? The stolen items might have been sold to them."

"There ain't none in East Anglia," the boy replied. "But there's one in London. The most famous is the Hall of Magic on the Isle of Man. Well, I'd better be off."

Climbing out the window, Nip disappeared.

"What do you make of that?" Joe asked his brother.

"I don't know. Why would anyone want to frame a boy like Nip? Unless it's just to distract attention from himself."

"But why would anyone try to make all this trouble in the artisan village? Whoever it is, he goes through quite a bit of effort with fire bombs and other equipment. It just doesn't make sense."

"Perhaps it's a crackpot who gets his kicks out of setting fires," Frank said.

At breakfast the next morning, Frank and Joe questioned Professor Rowbotham about the witch collection in London. He told them it was in Soho Square, not far from the Medmenham Book Store, so they could visit both the locksmith and the witch collection on one trip.

They decided to detour to the train station by way of Doctor Burelli's office so he could examine Joe's gum. The dentist reported that everything looked fine.

"Doc, I'm glad I have your vote of confidence," Joe declared. "We're going to London and I'd hate to get a toothache in the big city."

"I've something you might like to have," the dentist replied. Opening the trap door behind the dental chair, he climbed down into his workshop. A moment later he reappeared with a couple of masks. The dentist had a droll expression on his face.

"I detect you detectives are mystified. Well, the Gravesend Players wore these masks onstage last night. I have no further use for them. You might wear them next Halloween, back in the United States."

He handed one each to Frank and Joe. They were stretch-type rubber masks with a skin-tight fit. The features were those of two freckle-faced youths.

"The actors portrayed Scottish boys of about your age," Burelli explained.

The Hardys slipped the masks on and stared at the dentist.

"A perfect fit," he said. "You could fool your own mother, not to mention the criminals you keep under surveillance."

The boys pulled the masks off and pocketed them.

"Thanks," Joe said. "Could we fool a witch?"

Burelli became serious. "I don't know about a witch. But there's talk about what you're up to in Griffinmoor. The Gravesend Players were discussing you backstage last night. They know you were at John Pickenbaugh's funeral and are investigating the burglary at the Witch Museum."

"What do you think?" Frank queried.

Burelli grinned. "I think you two cover a lot of ground in one big hurry. Better be cautious."

Another patient needed attention, so they left the office and caught the London train.

On arriving, they quickly located Soho Square, the international district of the city. They heard languages from French to Arabic. Chinese merchants peered out of dingy windows. Spanish sailors sauntered past. North African gold speculators conversed among themselves, and sleazy-looking characters buttonholed easy marks.

"Frank, I have a notion we could buy anything illegal in Soho," Joe remarked. "Stolen gems, hijacked TV sets——"

"Forged passports," Frank finished the sentence. "But there's Marshall Street and the Medmenham Book Store, and a sign that says *Lock-smith.* That's what we want."

A small bell over the door tinkled as they stepped inside. The locksmith was a large, heavy-set, jolly man, who guffawed when they showed him their plaster cast.

"That's no key! It must have been a piece of scrap the masons dropped into the concrete when it was poured. And even if it was a key, the cast is too rough to work with."

Frank and Joe could not convince him to try to make a key. But they did peek into his work-shop because the door was ajar. They were fasci-nated by a suit of armor.

The locksmith noticed their interest. He said jovially, "Boys, how about minding the shop for me? I have to step out for a minute. Be my guests and look around."

They eagerly agreed. As soon as he left, they pushed the door open and went into the work-shop. A remarkable sight met their eyes.

There were several suits of medieval armor. A pair of crossed swords hung on the wall. A cross-bow stood in a corner, cocked and ready to fire a steel-tipped arrow. A headsman's ax lay on the floor, its wicked blade gleaming in the dim light of a small window overhead. A battleax was bal-anced in a vise with a file beside it. Darts and daggers littered the workbench.

Joe stood spellbound. "Frank, this guy must be hipped on medieval weapons!"

"I'd say he knows as much about them as Richard the Lion-Hearted. He should have been a crusader. Isn't there anything besides weapons in this room?"

Just then a noise made them stiffen. *Click!* The door snapped into place behind them. Whirling, Joe seized the knob and strove to wrestle the lock open. It refused to budge.

"Frank!" he exclaimed. "We're locked in! We're trapped!"

CHAPTER VIII

The Fortuneteller

FRANK placed the plaster cast for the key on the workbench and tried the door. Like Joe, he failed to get it open.

"What's up?" he wondered.

"Maybe it's somebody's idea of a joke," Joe said.

Frank looked worried. "I think the locksmith is trying to scare us, or something worse."

"Like what?"

"Like keep us prisoners!"

Joe whistled. "How do we get out of here?"

They inspected the room. The only exit besides the door was the overhead window.

"A bat couldn't get through that," Joe grumbled.

"Right," Frank said. "But I've got an idea!" Rapidly he explained his plan. "I hope it works," he concluded.

"Might as well give it a try, Frank."

They quietly slipped into two suits of armor. The metal felt cold, and the joints creaked as they pushed their hands down the arms into the gauntlets. Now they were completely covered, from the helmets on their heads down to the greaves on their legs and the iron shoes on their feet.

Joe picked up a spiked ball of the type used in medieval battles.

"Ready, Frank?"

"All set!"

Joe lobbed the ball up in the air and sent it through the window with a crash, showering broken glass and chips of splintered wood.

They heard it bounce on the pavement outside. There was a sound of rushing feet and a loud buzz of voices.

"My basketball set shot," Joe whispered.

"Quiet!" Frank warned. "Someone's coming."

A key turned in the lock. The door swung open and the locksmith lumbered into the room. The boys' eyes followed him as he searched around. Paying no attention to the suits of armor, he halted a few feet from the Hardys.

Frank held his breath. Joe wrinkled his nose and just managed to stifle a sneeze.

The locksmith looked up at the shattered window, a stunned expression on his face. Then he rushed out and they heard the tinkle of the bell on the front door.

"He's gone!" Frank exclaimed. "Come on! We've got to move fast!"

Climbing out of his suit of armor, Frank headed for the door. Joe called urgently after him.

"Wait a minute! I'm stuck!" Joe could not get his foot past the greave on the left leg. Frank ran back and held it, while his brother struggled to work himself loose.

"Wiggle your toes," Frank advised. "Hurry!"

Joe finally eased his foot free. "Boy! Am I glad to be out of that iron overcoat!"

They ran into the front room of the locksmith's establishment and out the door. At the corner they peeked around to the rear of the building, where a crowd was gathered.

People were milling about and pointing toward the smashed window. The owner stood holding the spiked ball in his hand and scratching his head in disbelief.

"Let him try to figure it out," Frank said.

"My guess is he never will." Joe chuckled. "His suspects are two suits of armor. And they ain't talking."

"Well, how about some refreshments? I'm starved."

"Good thinking."

They went into a teashop and ordered tea and

cakes. When the last of the food had vanished, Joe said, "Any idea what our pal the locksmith really had in mind?"

"He may be in cahoots with Matthew Hopkins," Frank theorized. "Hopkins may be the guy who's wearing the black hat. He could have called ahead and ordered the locksmith to take care of —oh—for Pete's sake!"

"What's the matter?"

"I left the cast of the key!"

"There goes our clue!"

"If it was a clue, the locksmith will have smashed it by this time," Frank said.

Joe nodded. "No use to go back. We might as well concentrate on our next project. Let's go see the Soho witch collection."

They paid their bill and walked down the block, mingling with the throngs who were out for the afternoon. A tout tried to sell the Hardys some black-market money, and quickly moved on when Frank said they were not interested. A sailor, who looked as if he had just jumped ship, followed them and stepped into a pub when he realized that they had noticed him.

"In Soho, there's no telling who's keeping you under surveillance," Frank noted.

"That's a good enough reason to hurry up and get out," Joe said.

They passed the Medmenham Book Store again and came to a window filled with amulets, such as bronze necklaces designed to save the wearer from the evil eye. A sign on the door read: WITCHCRAFT EXHIBITION.

Joe followed Frank through the revolving door. A number of rooms extended before them, crowded with shelves and display cases laden with objects similar to those described in Professor Rowbotham's Witch Museum catalog.

An old woman was seated at a small table near the door opposite an empty chair. She had a craggy face, piercing black eyes, and a long crooked nose. The boys noticed she wore a bronze bracelet on her left arm, a red comb in her black hair, and a silk robe studded with shooting stars.

"A fortuneteller," Frank murmured. "I wonder where she keeps the marked deck."

As if reading his mind, the old crone called out, "I am a palmist. I read palms and interpret what I see there. Let me read yours. I never lie."

"You might make a mistake," Joe teased her.

"Never, oh unbeliever. I am the last of a long line of witches. I know the wisdom of the ages. Trust me!"

"The whole point," Frank thought, "is that we don't trust you." Aloud he said, "Some other time."

The palmist glared as the boys strolled past and began to work their way around the witch collection room-by-room. A number of items appeared to be identical with those pictured in Rowbotham's catalog. One was a silver wand with a gold handle. Another was a crystal ball on a bronze tripod.

Frank rubbed his chin. "Joe, those could be part of the loot taken from the Griffinmoor museum."

"You're on my wavelength, Frank. I'd say this calls for a conference with the curator. He has some explaining to do."

Returning to the first room, they asked the palmist where they could find the curator of the exhibition.

"He's out for tea," she cackled. "So, you must wait. Why not pass the time letting me read your palms. You have nothing to lose, have you?"

"I guess not," Frank admitted.

Joe sat down in the empty chair and extended his hand. The woman took it in hers and examined his palm for a long time.

Suddenly she broke the silence with a loud "Hah! This is very interesting!"

"What is?" Joe inquired.

"This pattern of the lines of your palm. It tells me you have witch ancestry in your blood."

"Not bloody likely," Joe quipped.

"Do not scoff, young man. There is more. Let me see. Yes! Yes! Your life line is extremely short. Prepare yourself for sudden death if you proceed on your present course!"

Joe shivered in spite of himself and said he had

heard enough. Frank took the chair. The palmist surveyed his hand.

"You are haunted by a witchmaster," she informed him.

"Has he got a name?" Frank asked.

"The letters are here in your palm. I can read them. *P-I-C-K-E-N-B-A-U-G-H*. That is correct. His name is John Pickenbaugh."

Frank started when he heard the name. The woman clutched his hand tightly.

"You had better leave England," she intoned. "You are in grave danger!"

Frank tried to pull his hand away, but she kept clinging to it. Giving a sudden twist, she pressed something as sharp as a needle into his palm.

The room swam before his eyes. The face of the palmist became dim. Frank tried to say something to Joe but the words refused to come.

Abruptly he keeled over!

CHAPTER IX

Jumpy Sleuths

As Frank toppled, Joe caught his brother and eased him onto the floor. Frank lay still. His face was deathly pale and his breath came in gasps.

"Frank!" Joe shouted. "Can you hear me?"

Receiving no reply, he whirled around to confront the palmist. She was gone! The slow turning of the revolving door showed where she had exited during the confusion.

Desperately Joe hastened out onto the street and began calling for a doctor. A man with a medical bag answered and offered his assistance. Joe dragged Frank into the witch exhibition, where he lay motionless.

The doctor felt Frank's pulse and raised his eyelids for an examination of the pupils. Then he took a syringe from his bag and gave the boy an injection.

"Your brother has been drugged," the doctor

informed Joe. "But he'll be all right in a moment."

Frank began to breathe more easily. He regained consciousness, opened his eyes, and sat up, rubbing the back of his neck and shaking his head.

"What happened?" he asked groggily. "Oh, yes. Now I remember. I was having my palm read when the Empire State Building landed on me."

He struggled to his feet just as the curator of the witch collection arrived. He demanded to know what was going on in his establishment.

Joe quickly explained about the palmist. "She disappeared," he concluded ruefully.

"What can you tell us about her?" Frank asked.

"Very little," the curator said. "She arrived only this morning. Said she could read palms and would amuse the visitors to the witch exhibition. I gave her permission. I should have checked her references before doing so."

"Do you know where she lives?" Joe asked.

The curator shook his head. "I didn't see why I should ask."

Frank grimaced. "She must have been lying in wait for us. And we walked into her trap!"

"The spider invited the fly into her parlor," Joe joked. "Only this time it was a couple of flies, Frank. You and me."

The curator looked surprised. "If that was her game, you boys must have made her angry. What's your business in London?"

The Hardys confessed they were detectives working on the Griffinmoor case. They inquired whether the curator knew about the burglary in the Witch Museum.

He said he hadn't heard of it because he had been on vacation in France until the day before.

"Well," Frank pointed out, "you have quite a few items in this collection that look as if they had come from Griffinmoor." He described the wand and the crystal ball.

The curator slapped his forehead in dismay. "I bought these articles only yesterday. A man brought them in and said they were family heirlooms. I couldn't reject them. They are authentic witch equipment that once belonged to Matthew Hopkins, the Witchfinder General of East Anglia. Of course I will return them if they were stolen."

Frank saw a chance to pick up another clue. "Can you describe the man who sold you these objects?"

The curator nodded. "He was of medium height. He wore a long robe, had a heavy shock of gray hair, and a bushy beard."

Frank and Joe exchanged startled glances. The description fit the leader of the witches at John Pickenbaugh's funeral! The man who carried the sword!

Frank signaled Joe not to reveal their suspicion. He told the curator they would make a report to

Professor Rowbotham. Then they thanked him and left.

They walked out of Soho and across London's Piccadilly Circus to Green Park. There they sat down on a bench for a review of the case.

Joe tapped a knuckle against his chin. "Who can the palmist be, Frank? And why did she drug you?"

"My guess is that she used the needle when she couldn't scare us off," Frank said. "But how did she know where to wait for us? Who knew we were going to London today?"

"Professor Rowbotham."

"Check," Frank went on. "Who else?"

"Our buddy Dr. Burelli. And don't forget Sears," Joe said emphatically. "He knows we're on the Griffinmoor case, and he listens at keyholes."

Frank nodded slowly. "We'd better keep a close eye on him."

"Anyway, we picked up three more clues," Joe said. "First, the stolen articles. They might lead us to the thief."

"Second," Frank said, "there's the guy who sold them to the curator—alias the witch leader at the Pickenbaugh funeral."

"Third," Joe added, "there's the palmist. She might break the case wide open if only we could find her. Let's get this info down in writing and see how it shapes up."

They took out their notebooks with the pages headed "crimes," "suspects," "clues," and "theories," and filled in the facts of the Griffinmoor case.

The Hardys resumed their analysis of the mystery until they began to have a strange feeling that they were being spied on. Frank quickly looked in one direction and Joe in the other.

Under his breath Frank warned, "There's a man watching us. He's too far off to identify. But he's keeping us under surveillance. Anybody on your side?"

"Yes. A fat woman. I don't know who she is, either. But she's got a bead on us with opera glasses."

"Being spied on from opposite directions makes me jumpy," Frank muttered.

Suddenly it seemed as if all the people in Green Park were staring at the Hardys. A nurse wheeled a baby carriage in their direction. An elderly man holding an armful of books peered quizzically over his horn-rimmed spectacles. Faces appeared and vanished behind bushes and trees like mocking ghosts.

Joe shook himself. "I'm as jumpy as you are, Frank. Shall we go?"

"Okay by me."

"Suppose the man and woman follow us," Joe said.

"We'll have to give them the slip somehow. Come on!"

They got up and strolled down the street. "Let's stop in front of the display window of that shoe store there," Joe suggested. "Maybe we can see their reflections."

Frank nodded and casually pretended to examine the shoes in the window. The man and woman were still behind them!

"Oh, great," Joe muttered. "How about the department store across the street? Maybe we can lose them by leaving through a back door."

The boys went in and hurried through an aisle toward the rear. No luck! There was only one entrance! As they walked out, they noticed the couple on the other side of the street.

"They knew we had to come out here and just waited for us," Frank said. "Joe, I have an idea on how to get rid of them. Follow me!"

He led the way to a subway station, where they bought tickets for the *underground* at a vending machine. Hurrying to the escalator, they descended to the bottom. About ten yards opposite them, the up escalator was moving people toward the top exit.

Frank and Joe turned a corner at the bottom. They were alone.

"Quick!" Frank said. "Put on Burelli's mask!"

In moments both boys were transformed from

visiting Americans into freckle-faced Scottish youths.

Frank turned the corner again with Joe on his heels. This time they stepped onto the up escalator. The man and woman from the park were on the other side, going down behind a crowd of riders. Frank and Joe looked at them. They returned the gaze without recognizing their quarry.

At the bottom, the pair hurried toward the train. At the top, Frank stepped over to the down escalator.

"You're not going down again!" Joe blurted.

"Why not?"

"Pretty risky."

"Joe, they don't know us from Adam. And it's time to get to the station."

Riding to the bottom, they mingled with the Londoners waiting there. The man and woman had already gone along the platform and were looking through the crowd, when the train rattled in. It came to a standstill and the doors opened. The Hardys got on board. Some minutes later, safely on their way back to the train station, they chuckled over their strategy.

"We really fooled them," Joe said.

Frank nodded. "We should give Doc Burelli our special thanks!"

Before they had dinner aboard the train to Griffinmoor, the boys removed their masks and

"Quick!" Frank said. *"Put on Burelli's mask!"*

pondered the underground chase to see if they could make sense of it. Neither of them had been able to get a good look at the man. But they agreed that they could pick the woman out of a police lineup.

"She had the most piercing eyes I've ever seen," Joe said.

It was dark when they got off the train at Griffinmoor, but a lurid red glare suffused the sky to the east.

"A fire!" Frank exclaimed. "A four alarmer for sure! Looks as if Eagleton Green is going up in flames!"

CHAPTER X

A Wild Ride

A FIRE engine rumbled past, its bell clanging loudly.

"Let's follow it!" Joe exclaimed.

"Right. If there's been any more sabotage at Eagleton Green, we'd better investigate."

By the time the boys reached the scene, firemen were getting the blaze under control. A dozen shops had been damaged and their owners, who had congregated in the street, appeared to be stunned by the disaster.

Frank addressed the fire chief. "How did it start?"

"We don't know yet. But it looks suspicious."

While scouting around the area, the Hardys noticed that Lance McKnight's locksmith shop was barely scorched even though it stood between two badly charred buildings.

"That's strange," Joe said. "The fire burned

through the silversmith's shop, jumped over McKnight's, and landed right on the weaver's next door."

Frank shrugged doubtfully. "I wonder if it's a coincidence, Joe. If McKnight set the fires, he'd make sure he escaped."

"That figures."

McKnight was working with the firemen. He held the nozzle of a hose and played cascades of water over the burning buildings. Seeing Frank and Joe, he swiveled toward them.

The powerful stream of water hit Frank in the chest. He was knocked off his feet and sent skidding. Joe got the same treatment.

Drenched, bruised, and shaken, the boys rose to face McKnight, who had given the hose to a fireman and run to his victims.

"I'm sorry. I'm so sorry," he said effusively. "It was an accident. Really it was."

"So was the London blitz!" Joe said angrily.

"The hose got out of control," McKnight insisted.

"Okay. Forget it," Frank said.

McKnight seemed relieved, and he went into the silversmith's shop, where the fire chief was inspecting the damage.

"Well, he's a cool customer!" Frank exploded.

Joe shook the water from his clothes. "He did that deliberately. We've got a score to settle with Mr. McKnight."

Filtering through the crowd of Eagleton Green craftsmen, the Hardys kept their ears open. They learned that the fire just about ruined the artisan village and its residents.

"I'm ready to sell out," a jeweler stated. "The thefts in the past few months were bad enough, but the fire is the last straw. Start packing, say I!"

"Aye! Aye!" his neighbors shouted.

The village bookbinder raised his voice. "What's the reason for this harassment? Tell me that if you can!"

"Witchcraft!" a potter bellowed. "The robbery at the Witch Museum in Griffinmoor! It let the spirits of the witches loose! The spirits are haunting us!"

"That's right!" said a woman. "There's a lot of haunting around Eagleton Green! Pigs are dying, and no one knows why! Horses are falling sick, and the vets can't cure them!"

"Sure!" another agreed. "If it ain't witchcraft, what is it?"

It was depressing to listen to the crestfallen artisans. It appeared that Eagleton Green would not survive.

"Frank, look who's coming," Joe said as Professor Rowbotham weaved through the crowd toward them. Puffing, he swung his cane in a wide arc that barely missed Joe, who leaned back to avoid being hit.

"Ah—ah, I am pleased to have found you. I

thought you might be—ah—interested in the fire. I came here in the hope of running into you."

"What's up, professor?" Frank inquired.

"I have a message for the pair of you. It might help your investigation, but it is not something to—ah—discuss here. Suppose we go home. I have my car."

At his house, Rowbotham explained that an unidentified man had phoned to say he had vital information about the burglary at the Griffinmoor Witch Museum.

Joe became excited. "What kind of information is it? Does he have a suspect for us?"

"He refused to say. Indeed—ah—he told me he has sworn an oath never to reveal what he knows about the burglary."

Frank looked crestfallen. "So, a guy tells you he's got the info, and then he tells you he's not telling."

Rowbotham blinked. "Not exactly. I mean, he said he might be released from his oath under certain conditions."

Frank perked up. "What conditions?"

"Ah—ah, he wants a meeting at Stonehenge."

"You mean," Joe said, "where the cave men tossed those boulders around like marbles?"

Rowbotham smiled. "I imagine we are talking about the same place. Yes, Stonehenge, where prehistoric people placed those—ah—massive stone blocks in a precise arrangement.

"The Druids used Stonehenge for their religious rituals. The man who phoned said he could speak freely at the Druid altar when the full moon is in the sky. To wit—tomorrow night!"

Joe chuckled. "Sounds like a lot of hocus-pocus to me. I'm not a Druid!"

"The man might know something," Rowbotham said solemnly. "He might be a witch!"

"Or pose as one," Frank remarked. "This could be a setup."

Rowbotham looked puzzled. "A setup? I am not familiar with the term."

"A trap," Frank interpreted.

"He might want to ambush us," Joe said, "down where the Druids play."

Rowbotham looked dubious. "Ah—ah, I think we should take the risk. My informant might unravel the mystery for us. At least you boys will see Stonehenge. I'll be your guide to the ruins."

The three talked it over, and the Hardys at last agreed to go. Rowbotham said he would drive them the hundred miles or so to Stonehenge, and they could return to Griffinmoor immediately if the man did not appear.

"Now, then, what have you to report about your visit to London?" the professor inquired.

Frank described their adventures in Soho. "So you see," he ended, "we were locked in by a locksmith and then I was drugged by this palmist who was supposed to be telling me my fortune."

Joe took up the story, covering their stop in Green Park and the underground surveillance.

"What do you propose to do about these hostile persons?" Rowbotham asked.

"We could prosecute the locksmith," Joe said.

"No good," Frank retorted. "We don't have any proof. I'd sure like to corral that palm reader, though."

Rowbotham suggested a phone call to the London police. Frank agreed and conversed for a few minutes with the officer at the desk. Hanging up, he rejoined Joe and the professor.

"The police don't know anything about the palmist," he said. "She's not local. They've got plenty of fortunetellers in their mug books, but none of them sounded like the gal with the needle."

Joe mentioned the items in the London witch collection that seemed to have been taken from the Griffinmoor museum.

"Ah—ah, the wand and the crystal ball were stolen from here," Rowbotham stated. "I myself discovered that they once belonged to the Witchfinder General, Matthew Hopkins. I am happy to know the curator is willing to return them. If only we could find the rest of the artifacts!"

Something clicked in Frank's mind. "Perhaps some of it was shipped out of England! Interest in witchcraft has revived all over the world. Traffic in the stolen objects could be international. Let's check with Interpol."

"And with Dad, too," Joe added.

"Ah—ah, I can give you a duplicate catalog for your father," Rowbotham offered.

They prepared an air-mail package along with a letter to their parents, and Rowbotham ordered Sears to post it.

Frank and Joe were tired when they went to bed. However, they were up early the next morning, eager to get on with the case.

At breakfast, a letter arrived from Fenton Hardy. He told his sons that their ancestors had emigrated to America from Dublin after the Salem witch trials. He also suggested they check on the Irish genealogy of the Hardy family if they had time, and he sent his regards to his old friend Chauncey Rowbotham.

"Your father should see how well you are doing," Rowbotham complimented Frank and Joe.

"Still, we haven't solved your case, professor," Frank said.

"Let's see if the Griffinmoor police are doing any better," Joe said.

He phoned local headquarters and asked about the Pickenbaugh grave robbery. He found that the police were at a dead end, without clues or suspects.

"They're putting John Pickenbaugh's case on the back burner," Joe said after hanging up.

"Might as well make tracks for Stonehenge," Frank concluded.

"We can ask the Druids to solve the case for us," Joe said humorously.

They went outside and got into the car to wait for Professor Rowbotham. He appeared, wearing a long white coat, a peaked white hat, a pair of thick goggles, and heavy gloves with broad leather cuffs.

"My driving costume," he explained to the Hardys, who were staring at him in bug-eyed amazement. "I never take a long ride without wearing my driving costume."

He turned on the engine, released the brake, and started with a jerky motion and a grating noise that sounded as if he were stripping the gears.

"Ah—ah, we are off!" he announced.

Off is right! Joe thought.

The Hardys began to worry as the compact barreled southwest out of Norfolk across the center of England toward Stonehenge. Professor Rowbotham wandered from one side of the road to the other. He ignored traffic signals. He went either too fast or too slow. And he chortled to himself as he drove.

Not far from their destination, Rowbotham ran over a duck as he whizzed past a farmhouse.

"The farmer will have a duck dinner," Frank muttered under his breath. He looked through the rear window. The duck had escaped between the wheels of the car and was waddling into the farmyard, quacking loudly.

On and on the compact sped. Just when Frank and Joe believed they would make it all the way to Stonehenge without an accident, Rowbotham swung across the road to pass the car in front of him. Unfortunately the other lane was occupied by a car being driven in the opposite direction at full speed.

Rowbotham gave his compact the gas in a frantic effort to get out of the way. It bucked, rocked, and skidded, as two wheels crunched onto a soft shoulder.

Out of control, the car careened into a ditch!

CHAPTER XI

The Stonehenge Caper

THE car jolted to a halt on the other side of the ditch. Frank's neck whiplashed, and Joe grabbed the dashboard to avoid being thrown against it.

Professor Rowbotham slumped over the steering wheel, a trickle of blood above his eye showing where he had struck his head.

Joe shook him. "Professor! Professor!"

Frank rubbed the back of his neck to ease the pain. "He's knocked out, Joe. Let's give him some first aid."

Frank ran around the car and Joe helped him edge Rowbotham from the driver's seat to the ground. Frank pulled out his handkerchief and wiped away the blood. "Just a little cut," he said.

Rowbotham groaned and opened his eyes.

"How are you?" Frank asked anxiously.

"Ah—ah, I have a headache. But—ah—I'm all right. How about the car?"

Joe got in, started the motor, and guided the vehicle back up onto the road.

"She's A-okay," he called out, "except for a dent in the fender."

"Ah—ah, then let's continue to Stonehenge," the professor said.

Frank looked doubtful. "Do you feel up to it? You have one big robin's egg over your eye."

"That doesn't bother me," Rowbotham said emphatically.

"It bothers me," Joe thought. He said aloud, "I'll drive if you like, Professor."

"Certainly not," Rowbotham replied testily. "I am quite capable of driving my car!"

They got in and resumed their journey, rolling through the counties of western England until they reached Wiltshire.

Rowbotham commented on the flatness of the terrain. "This is Salisbury Plain. Soon we will see Stonehenge. Ah—there it is!"

A group of tall stones came into view. They were arranged in a circle.

"We are now approaching the Avenue of Stonehenge," Rowbotham explained.

"Avenue?" Frank said curiously.

"Well, you see, the people who constructed Stonehenge built a thoroughfare up to it."

"The Druid Fifth Avenue," Joe chuckled. "Not as lively as New York, though."

Rowbotham spoke like a professor lecturing to

a class. "The Druids were not responsible for the Avenue. My goodness, no!"

"I thought the Druids built Stonehenge," Frank said in a puzzled tone.

"A popular misconception. Stonehenge goes back to the Stone Age. Ah—the Druids appeared much later. They lived here on Salisbury Plain in Roman times. However, it is true that they used the site for their ceremonies."

He turned the car into a parking area and stopped. The three got out and walked across the grass to the group of stones. A broad entrance led through a low embankment, curving away on each side. Rowbotham swung his cane in a wide arc, forcing Frank to duck out of its path.

"This is the outermost circle," he said. "The distance across to the other side of the circle is one hundred yards."

"As long as a football field," Frank noted.

"A ball carrier would have to do a lot of broken field running to reach the end zone," Joe quipped. "Jumbo blocks of granite for linebackers. What a defense!"

"Ah—I don't quite understand. Is that an American proverb?"

"Just football terminology," Frank told him.

Rowbotham walked down to the center of the circle. He tapped a stone with his cane. "There are, as I said before, two stone circles. The outer one has stones—ah—thirteen feet tall. Only about half are still standing, but you can imagine what it looked like when they were all in place."

He turned toward the largest blocks. "This is called the Horseshoe because five groups stood in a curve, with the open end facing the Avenue. The three still standing are more than twenty feet tall. They weigh—ah—over forty tons."

Frank and Joe tilted their heads back and glanced up. The rocks of the Horseshoe looked like menacing giant sentries.

"How did these Stone Age skyscrapers get here?" Joe wondered.

"A good question. The witches of old England said Merlin the Magician transported them through the air from Ireland. Modern archaeologists say they came from the stone pits of Marlborough Downs, twenty miles to the north. Ah—how prehistoric men moved such heavy objects remains a mystery."

Rowbotham tapped a single large slab lying in the center of Stonehenge. "This is the Altar Stone. Our Druids and witches still convene around it."

"So," Frank put in, "this is where the mystery man wants us to meet him."

"Precisely. That is why I suggest he may be a witch."

"He's off his rocker, if you ask me," Joe declared. "Druids! Who needs them!"

Rowbotham sighed. "I see you are skeptics who do not believe in Druids or witches. Our adventure tonight may change your minds. Ah—it is getting dark. We had better prepare for the meeting."

Suddenly he pressed his fingertips to his forehead, swayed, and leaned on his cane. The Hardys urged him to see a doctor about the bump he had received in the accident on the road. He refused.

"Ah—ah, we would have to go into the town of Salisbury, which would be a waste of time. Besides, I'm not badly hurt. I will rest in the car until I feel better."

Frank and Joe each braced one of his elbows and escorted him out of Stonehenge, along the Avenue, and back to the car. They carefully deposited him in the rear seat.

"Thank you," the professor said in a grateful tone. "I think I will take a nap. You can keep the appointment in Stonehenge, and I will wait for you to return. By the way, ah—Stonehenge means Hanging Stones."

He leaned back and closed his eyes.

"He's still woozy," Frank said.

"Well, there's nothing more we can do for him," Joe pointed out. "Come on!"

They retraced their steps along the Avenue and back to Stonehenge.

A fog was rising from Salisbury Plain, and a full moon hung in the night sky. The titanic monuments loomed stark, black, and sinister in its white glow. Narrow shafts of light filtered between them in eerie patterns. The only sound was the sobbing of the wind.

"I hope this guy doesn't stand us up," Frank said.

Suddenly they heard a musical note on the Avenue. It came closer, and the boys recognized it as the high register of a recorder, a flutelike instrument. They quickly ducked behind one of the Horseshoe stones and peered out.

"Holy cow!" Frank whispered. "Look at that!"

A long line of people came into view. Men and women were dressed alike in white robes and flowing white headdresses. Each carried a single flower in one hand.

"Who on earth are those people?" Joe asked.

"Druids, I guess!"

The marchers filed up to the Altar Stone and placed their flowers on it. Then they turned to face the full moon and began to chant.

> Druid magic, Druid lore,
> Be our guide as in days of yore.
> Stonehenge stones and pale moonlight,
> Guard our ritual tonight.

Joe shuddered as he listened to the strange chant. Frank, feeling his foot going to sleep, gave it a twist and accidentally kicked the stone.

"What was that?" one of the Druids called in a strident voice.

The leader, a burly man with a white beard, gazed around. The Hardys crouched low behind the stone. Their hearts thumped.

"An owl, no doubt," the leader said. "The bird of wisdom. It is fortunate that he takes note of our rite. Now, let us go."

The weird column filed out of Stonehenge and the sound of the recorder died away.

"Wow!" Frank said. "I'm glad they didn't notice us."

"They might not have taken kindly to intruders," Joe agreed.

"This is a good hiding place," Frank said. "We might as well stay here. When the guy arrives, I'll go out. You stay as a backup. Okay?"

"Roger."

They settled down to wait. The moon climbed higher in the sky. The wind blew harder. The fog grew denser.

"I can't see the altar any more," Frank said after a while. "Let me find a good spot closer to it. When I do, I'll come for you."

"Right."

Frank slipped away into the mist. Five minutes passed. Joe became apprehensive. Had anything happened to his brother? He waited five minutes more, then he could stand it no longer. He crept out of his hiding place in the direction of the altar. There was no sign of Frank. Joe searched all around it.

"Frank," he called in a low voice. "Frank, where are you?"

He heard a rustle behind him and whirled around. "Frank——?"

A white-hooded figure aimed a punch at his neck. He ducked in time. The man attacked him again, and the two wrestled in the dark. Joe's adversary was powerful and agile. He gave Joe a punch to the jaw that jarred him back against the Altar Stone. The boy dodged a second swing, and the man's fist hit the stone with a crunch. He groaned and backed off, breathing heavily through his mask.

Suddenly a second hooded figure appeared out of the fog. He forced Joe back onto the stone and began to choke him. With a superhuman effort, Joe struck back with a chop under the man's chin. He gulped and let go.

Joe sat up groggily. He noticed the man clutching his jaw, and tried to figure out a way to escape. There was none. The other fellow, who had hurt his hand, now closed in on him. Joe raised his arms in self-defense; then an eerie sound pierced the night air. Was it a note on the recorder of the Druids?

It made the boy shiver. The two men looked at each other, and one motioned to the other to run. They raced past the monuments and vanished into the fog of Salisbury Plain.

"Wow!" Joe said to himself. "Whatever that

sound was, it certainly saved me!" He stood up, still breathing hard. If only he could find his brother!

"Frank," he called in a low voice. "Frank, where are you?"

No answer. Joe cautiously moved in the dense fog. "Frank!" he repeated.

Suddenly he heard a low moan. "Hey, Frank?"

"Here," came the faint reply.

Joe felt his way in the darkness until he reached his brother's prone figure. "Are you all right?" he asked anxiously. "What happened?"

Frank sat up and shook his head. "I got kayoed by an apparition in a hood."

"I almost did, too. It was a trap after all."

"Did you see who it was?"

"No. Two men. They disappeared this way," Joe said, pointing.

"No sense in following them in this fog," Frank said. "We might as well go to the car." He got to his feet.

As they turned to go back to the professor's compact, Joe tripped over something soft. "Hey, what's this?" he said. He picked up a striped cap and handed it to Frank.

"This looks like the cap Nip Hadley wears," Frank exclaimed.

"Right. I wonder if he was one of that gruesome twosome."

Frank turned the cap inside out. In the moonlight he read the label. The cap came from a store on the Isle of Man. They decided this was a clue they would investigate when they got the chance.

"Perhaps we should go there," Frank said.

They trotted back to the parking area where they had left Rowbotham in his car. It was deserted. There was no sign of the auto. The professor was gone!

CHAPTER XII

Mysterious Message

JOE scratched his head. "I wonder where the prof is!"

"Search me. Looks like he vamoosed on us," Frank said. "Think he's a phony? Maybe he knew those guys were waiting for us. That would explain why he was so dead set on getting us to Stonehenge."

"Could be. But why? Perhaps that bump on his head was acting up and he went to a doctor. Let's check."

They jogged into town, where they went to police headquarters. The officer on duty shook his head when they described Rowbotham. No such person had been reported injured.

The Hardys next tried the Salisbury hospital. The reply was negative there, too. No patient had come in to have a bump over his eye treated.

Frank and Joe walked to Salisbury's main street.

"Lost—one professor!" Joe said, worried.

Frank, too, was solemn. "We'd better get back to Griffinmoor as soon as possible, if there's a train at this time of night."

The station was dark and deserted when they arrived. A schedule told them the next train to Griffinmoor did not leave until the following noon.

"Too bad we don't have a broomstick to ride back to the witch museum!" Joe grumbled.

"We could try our thumbs," Frank suggested.

Glumly they walked to the highway, trying to hitch a ride. Finally a car stopped. The driver was about their age. He said he was a student and would give them a lift as far as Oxford.

"Fine," Frank told him. "It's on the route to Griffinmoor. That's where we're going."

As they drove along, the three discussed the differences between England and America. The sun had risen by the time the spires of Oxford came into view. The Hardys got out, thanked their driver, and began thumbing again.

At Bedford, a large Lincoln Continental pulled to the side of the highway to wait for them. Eagerly they ran to it.

The driver was a stout motherly woman, who wore an enormous hat that resembled a bowl of fruit. Around her neck was a large fox fur. She invited them to get in and started up again. Frank and Joe explained they were traveling from Salisbury to Griffinmoor.

"All the way from Salisbury!" the woman said sympathetically. "And all night on the road! You poor boys must be tired!"

"I could be more lively," Frank admitted.

"And I'm not about to do any handstands either," Joe said. Then he added, "Where are you going, ma'am?"

"Home!"

"Home?" the Hardys queried in unison.

"Yes. You boys need a bath, a meal, and a nap. My house is just the place. When you feel fit, you can resume your journey."

Frank and Joe were alarmed at the thought of any delay in their investigation.

"Where's home, ma'am?" Frank inquired.

"Johnshire. Only about twenty-five miles out of your way. We should be there in an hour."

"Well, that's very kind of you, but you see, we have to be in Griffinmoor at a certain time and——"

"Nonsense! Wherever you have to be, you won't be any good if you're tired out. Nothing's as important as a good rest."

"We've been resting in the car," Frank protested weakly. "Right now, I feel like a million dollars!"

"And I'm ready to do handsprings like crazy!" Joe boasted.

"You're just saying that," the woman objected. "I know. I have three sons of my own. I understand what boys need. You're coming home with me. I won't take no for an answer."

The Hardys became desperate. They urged her to drop them off. She repeated that they had to be spruced up after being awake all night. They insisted they did not want to be any trouble. The smiling woman replied that they would not be any trouble at all.

She kept on driving, and they wondered how to escape from the motherly grip of their good Samaritan. They were beginning to give up hope when she slowed her car to turn off the main road. Frank made a split-second decision. He nudged Joe with his elbow, a signal to get ready for action.

As the nose of the car began to turn the corner, Frank wrenched the door open and flung himself out. Joe piled out after him. They hit the turf alongside the highway, tumbled over, and scrambled to their feet.

"Whew! That was a close call!" Joe gasped.

They saw the car stop halfway up the side street. It began to back toward them!

"She thinks we fell out!" Frank cried. "Make tracks before she corrals us again!"

They raced up the highway and caught another

ride in the nick of time. This driver took them into Cambridge and left them standing on the sidewalk in front of a grilled gateway. A plaque read: DOWNING COLLEGE.

"I'd like to see the Cambridge colleges," Joe remarked.

"So would I," Frank answered. "But we don't have time."

A lorry rattled down the road. The driver said he could take them as far as Griffinmoor.

"Great!" Joe said as they climbed up.

They reached the Rowbotham house, feeling tired, dirty, and discouraged. Joe punched the doorbell, and Sears gasped when he opened up.

"What's the matter?" Frank asked him. "Did you expect us to stay in Stonehenge permanently?"

"Oh, no sir," the butler responded. "It is simply that Professor Rowbotham has been wondering where you were."

It was the Hardys' turn to stare. "You mean the professor is here?" Joe exclaimed.

"Yes sir. He is waiting for you."

"How long has he been back?" Frank wanted to know.

"Long enough to become angry with you, I'm afraid."

They found Rowbotham sitting in an easy chair in the study. He had his hands cupped over

They hit the turf alongside the highway!

the handle of his cane. The bump on his head was still there.

"What did you mean, leaving me alone at Stonehenge?" he scowled.

"I beg your pardon, sir," Frank said. "You were the one who did the leaving! Why did you drive home without us?"

"But you sent me a message saying that you weren't coming back with me!"

"What?"

"Oh dear, now I see. It must have been a deception. Tell me, what happened to you?"

After hearing them out, the professor looked embarrassed. "Ah—ah, I must apologize for blaming you," he said. "The fact is that a man came along while I was asleep in the car. He woke me up."

"What did he look like?" Frank asked.

"He had a heavy shock of ah—gray hair. Also a bushy beard."

Frank and Joe looked at each other. The description fitted the leader of the witch mourners at the funeral of John Pickenbaugh!

"The man," Rowbotham went on, "told me he had a message from you boys."

"What was it?" Joe asked.

"He said you had picked up an important clue, and had gone off to investigate it. He said you wanted me to drive back to Griffinmoor alone."

"That was a lie!" Joe informed him. "We would never have told you to drive over a hundred miles when you were woozy from that blow on the head!"

Rowbotham nodded. "I can see that now. But at the time, I thought you had met the man who phoned here. I supposed he had given you vital information about the burglary at the Witch Museum."

"That's understandable," Frank said soothingly. "But how did you manage to drive to Griffinmoor?"

"Ah—ah, by that time I felt rested. Had a bit of trouble starting the car, but the man was very kind and helped me."

"I bet he was kind!" Frank muttered.

"Well, ah—ah, I suppose I should have suspected him. Not very perceptive at all. Sorry about that."

"Don't worry," Joe said. "We made it back okay."

"Ah—ah, I am glad you did. Now I'll go to my room and take a nap."

Sears helped him up the stairs. Frank and Joe went outside to make sure the butler would not hear them. They stopped by a rosebush to discuss the new turn of events.

"I suspect the prof," Joe asserted. "Why didn't he try to find us in Stonehenge?"

"And was he really as dizzy as he pretended?" Frank mused. "Or is he fuzzing up the facts to keep us in the dark? What'll we do now?"

"The car, Frank! Maybe it'll tell us more than the prof did."

They went into the garage and searched the compact. Joe had his head in the trunk when Frank called him in an excited voice. He was in the driver's seat. As Joe approached, Frank handed him a cablegram.

"Take a gander at this! I found it wedged between the two front seats!"

Joe opened the cablegram. It was from New York. The message read: *Plans changed. Get rid of Hardys.*

CHAPTER XIII

A Near Miss

Joe whistled. "Somebody's awfully careless with his cables!"

"That's for sure. This is one hot item to leave where we can find it. Any ideas off the top of your head, Sherlock?"

Joe hazarded a guess. "The cablegram was dropped when Bushy Beard helped the prof start his car in Stonehenge. Now we know for sure somebody's out to get us. And he's got a partner in the good old U.S.A."

Frank reflected for a moment. "If Bushy Beard dropped it accidentally, then he's our enemy, not the professor."

"Still, I think we should ask point-blank if the cable belongs to him," Joe said.

"All right. His reaction might give us a clue."

The clatter of horses' hooves announced the arrival of Nip Hadley. The Craighead groom rode

Midnight up the semicircular driveway and drew rein. The Hardys joined him. They noticed he had a black eye and wasn't wearing his cap.

"Where'd you get the shiner, Nip?" Joe asked.

"Playing soccer."

"Why no cap?" Frank said.

"Left it in the stable." The groom quickly changed the subject. "I'm glad you blokes are here. I have news for you."

"Spill it, pal," Frank said.

Nip glanced around to see that nobody was listening. Then he bent down and whispered, "I was in the kitchen over at Craighead Castle. I heard someone mention your name. Not a friendly voice, either. I don't know who it was, but he could be an enemy of yours. You better watch out!"

"Looks as if we have enemies all over England," Joe joked.

"Also across the Atlantic," Frank continued.

"What are you driving at?" Nip seemed puzzled.

Before the Hardys could reply, a red MG eased into the driveway. Nip turned in the saddle to make sure the vehicle had enough room to pass his horse. Deciding it had, he looked again at his American friends.

The MG came up slowly until it was a few yards away. Suddenly the driver stepped on the gas. Gravel spun under the tires as the car powered forward.

The MG hurtled at Frank and Joe! They whirled and saw that the driver was wearing a mask. Instinctively the Hardys hit the ground behind Midnight, using the horse for a shield.

The sound of the advancing automobile frightened the animal. It reared and threw Nip out of the saddle. He landed on the Hardys, and all three lay sprawled in the driveway.

The MG careened past like a red flash and roared away in a cloud of dust.

Nip picked himself up and quieted his horse, while Frank and Joe got shakily to their feet. None of them had noticed the car's license plate.

"I saw an emblem of the London Motor Club," Joe reported. "At least it's a clue."

Nip remounted, wondering aloud why anybody would want to kill the Americans.

"That's for him to know and for us to find out!" Frank responded grimly. "By the way, Nip, can you arrange a tour of the castle for us? We'd like to see how the Craigheads live before we go back home."

Nip looked down in surprise. "When will that be?"

Frank gave Joe a sidelong wink, telling him to play along. "Pretty soon."

"Any day now," Joe agreed. "How about the tour?"

"Sorry. Ain't got th authority. I'm just in charge of the stable. You'll have to ask somebody who works inside the castle. Cheerio!"

Turning Midnight's head, Nip slapped the horse with his crop and cantered down the driveway. The clip-clop of horseshoes on gravel died away.

"This case is getting more mysterious all the time," Frank observed.

"And more dangerous," Joe warned. "Let's go in. We can talk to the prof when he wakes up. If he knows anything about the cablegram, he'd better come clean."

Sears informed them that Rowbotham was awake and in the study. The murmur of voices told them a visitor had arrived. As they approached the room, they recognized the caller's voice. It was Dr. Burelli.

"There's only one way for us to solve the problem," the dentist was saying, "and that is to get rid of——" He broke off upon noticing Frank and Joe.

Rowbotham invited the boys into the study.

"My patient and his brother," Burelli greeted them. "How do your gums feel, Joe?"

"Fine," Joe said. "No problem."

"No pain?"

"None."

"Ah—ah, we were discussing the Gravesend Players," Rowbotham interjected. "One actor wants to play a lead role that he is simply incompetent to handle."

"Fancies himself as Hamlet," Burelli stated "but he should stick to Peter Pan. As I came in the back way, I spied you talking to Nip Hadley. You seem to be friends with him now. He's not a bad chap when you get to know him."

"Nip's got a few rough edges," Frank said. "That's all."

"The groom needs grooming." Burelli laughed.

"We asked him if we could tour the castle," Frank went on, "but he said he didn't have the authority to let us in. Only someone who works in the place could."

"Ah—ah, Sears' sister is married to Goodman, the Craighead butler," Rowbotham said. "Perhaps he could arrange it for you."

"That would be great!" Joe said.

The professor rang for his servant and requested that he ask his sister about the matter.

"Certainly, sir," Sears replied. "I am sure we can do it. My sister is the housekeeper at the castle and will be glad to take you around. I'll go along to make sure everything is in order."

The boys were galvanized. "How about tomorrow, Sears?" Frank asked. "We would like to get a good night's rest before starting on that venture."

"Agreed, sir," Sears replied.

"Well, I must return to duty," Burelli informed the gathering.

Rowbotham escorted him to the front door. When he came back, Frank pulled the cablegram from his pocket and handed it to him.

"What is it?" the professor asked.

"Read it, sir."

Curiously Rowbotham glanced at the piece of paper. A look of alarm came over his face. "Ah—ah, that is—well, that is outrageous!"

"We thought so, too," Joe said.

"Where did you find it?"

"In your car!"

"What? Impossible! How would it get——"

The professor staggered over to his easy chair and collapsed in it.

CHAPTER XIV

The Curse

ALL the blood had drained from the professor's face. He looked ill.

Frank was alarmed. "You need to see a doctor, sir!"

Rowbotham shook his head. "Ah—ah, I did. He told me I had a mild concussion. Nothing to worry about."

Joe was suspicious. "Is the cablegram what's bothering you?"

"Just so. But I know—ah—nothing about it. I am concerned for your safety. Perhaps some evil person wants you out of the way because you are close to a solution of the burglary at the Witch Museum."

"We have made no headway," Joe scoffed. "This looks like one case we're not going to solve!"

"I have a feeling all these mysterious shenanigans are connected with Lord Craighead's disappearance," Frank said. "Was he really on his way to Dublin five years ago?"

Rowbotham shrugged. "Everybody in Griffinmoor believed he was. Nobody denied it at the time."

"It could have been a cover story he dreamed up," Joe pointed out. "Anyhow, there's one place to look for him."

"Where?" Rowbotham asked.

"Dublin!"

Frank nodded. "I go along with that. We'd better add Ireland to our transatlantic tour. Professor, suppose you spread the word that we've gone home. That way we can carry on the investigation without fear of anybody tailing us."

Rowbotham agreed. He told them to go to Tara Lodge near Dublin. "This is the home of Lord Craighead's army friend, Colonel Melvin Stewart. They were supposed to meet there."

The Hardys made their plans that night. They would visit Craighead Castle the next day, and on the following morning, fly to Dublin.

"I'll pack the cap we found at Stonehenge," Frank said. "Maybe we can go to the Isle of Man and check it out."

The following day they set out with Sears for the Craighead estate. Joe drove Rowbotham's compact through town and out into the countryside, while Frank mulled over the mysterious cablegram from New York. He put a pointed question to the butler.

"Sears, have you any relatives in America?"

"No, sir. But my brother-in-law, Mr. Goodman, has a cousin in New York. Why do you ask?"

Frank pretended to be unconcerned. "Just curiosity. Being Americans, we're interested in Englishmen who have relatives living in our country."

The tower of Craighead Castle appeared over the crest of a hill. Joe coasted down the grade, up the driveway, and across a drawbridge into the castle courtyard.

Goodman and his wife came out to greet them. He was short, they noticed, and she very thin. Cordially the couple escorted the visitors inside.

"Milton Craighead is in London," Mrs. Goodman confided. "So there's no fear of disturbing him. But first we will have tea in the drawing room."

She rang a silver bell. Two servants wheeled a cart in. They placed cups and a large teapot on the table along with a tray of cakes.

Joe noticed that the housekeeper had piercing black eyes. She kept glancing at him even while talking to the others. He felt very uncomfortable under her gaze, but decided to forget it and down his share of tea and cakes.

After refreshments the tour of the castle began. First they went into the dungeon. A small round window let in just enough light to reveal a dismal sight. There were torture instruments in the middle of the floor—thumbscrews, racks, and braziers for heating pincers. Irons for holding wrists and ankles dangled from a rafter. Cowhide whips were stacked in a wooden cask.

"Of course we don't use this room any more," Mrs. Goodman informed the Hardys. "But it had quite a bit of use in the olden times."

The boys were glad when the butler led the way up again into the living quarters. They went along corridors and saw rooms that still spoke of elegance and splendor, even though a time-worn shabbiness prevailed. Finally they reached the battlements. The embrasures once manned by archers were empty. The openings for pouring boiling oil on besieging armies were covered over.

"I guess Craighead Castle hasn't been in a scrap for a long time," Frank said.

"There hasn't been a battle for over three hundred years," Goodman replied.

The group ascended to the top of the tower, where a flag flew in the breeze. It bore a picture of a griffin carrying off a knight. Joe made out the legend: *Avoir la Serre Bonne.*

"The Griffinmoor emblem!" he exclaimed.

Mrs. Goodman fixed her black eyes on him.

"You are right—this time," was her cryptic response.

Before he could ask what she meant, the woman urged the group down the stairs from the tower and into the turret at the rear of the castle. The top room of the turret had no window. Explaining that the electricity had never been extended to the turret, Goodman lit a large candle and held it up high.

The flickering light fell upon an array of old armor. There was a Norman suit made of tiny bits of metal linked together. Behind it stood a French type, made of metal plates.

In one corner gleamed a suit of jet black armor holding a sword in one hand.

Frank patted the helmet. "So that's what the well-dressed knight wore."

"I hope he didn't feel itchy," Joe quipped. "How'd you like to try scratching your back through that tin outfit?"

The candle sputtered out. Goodman led them into the corridor. They descended into the courtyard and walked around the castle.

One thing struck Joe. Sunlight once more glinted off a window in the turret, but he could not remember seeing the window from within.

While pondering his oversight, they came to a wide stone staircase. Mrs. Goodman asked Frank to lead the way down. He did.

Zip! His feet skidded out from under him, and he plunged head over heels, bouncing from one step to another till he hit bottom. Joe rushed to help him up.

"What a terrible fall!" the housekeeper cried. "How did it happen?"

"I slipped on something!"

The Hardys and Sears examined the step and found a broad, dark, oozy discoloration.

"That's oil!" Sears exclaimed, rubbing some between his fingers.

"Goodness, how did it get there?" the woman asked.

Goodman insisted that he had no explanation for the oil. He promised to look into the matter and see if anyone in the castle was responsible, and begged Frank to accept his apologies.

"It's okay," Frank said. "I banged a knee and skinned an elbow. But I'm still operational."

The visit over, Joe drove back to Griffinmoor. Passing the tearoom in town, they were startled to see a figure in a polka-dot bandanna run out and jump in front of the car. Joe braked to a jarring stop.

"Mary Ellerbee!" he exclaimed.

The old crone pointed a bony finger at them.

"The witch's curse!" she shrieked. "The day will come when it is done! The deed is nigh, the witch's cry is heard on high. To you I say, avaunt!"

Gathering her robe about her, she strode back into her tearoom. The black cat leaped into her arms, and Mary Ellerbee stood in the doorway, stroking the pet and leering.

"What was that all about?" Frank wondered as Joe drove on.

"She's harmless," Sears said. "Pay no attention to her."

"Witches are great on curses," Joe murmured.

Mary's action bothered the Hardys, even though they kept telling each other that superstition was ridiculous.

Next morning they bade the professor good-by and took the train to London, where a taxi whisked them to the airport. With their baggage safely on the conveyor belt, Frank and Joe stopped at a lunch counter for coffee and doughnuts.

Frank looked at his watch. "We've got an hour till flight time. What say we phone home? It's noon here, so it's morning in Bayport."

"Good idea," Joe said. "Won't they be surprised!"

The call went through quickly, and their mother answered. She was delighted to hear their voices. "Professor Rowbotham must be a nice man." She sighed in relief after listening to their story of events in Griffinmoor.

Neither Frank nor Joe wanted to worry Mrs. Hardy by mentioning their suspicions about their host. Fenton Hardy came to the phone. His sons gave him a rapid rundown of their investigation.

"It's a bigger mystery than I thought," the Bayport sleuth confessed. "But Sam Radley has made a discovery at this end that might help you crack the case."

Sam Radley was Mr. Hardy's operative. He had helped Frank and Joe solve a number of crimes. They knew they could depend on him.

"What is it?" Frank urged.

"We could use an assist in this ball game," added Joe, who had his ear next to the receiver.

"Sam has been casing New York shops that specialize in the occult. He checked some items against the inventory you sent. They're from Professor Rowbotham's Witch Museum!"

"Holy catfish!" Joe exploded. "No wonder we couldn't find more of the stuff over here!"

"We thought this might be an international gang," Frank declared. "I guess our hunch wasn't far off."

"It was right on the money," Fenton Hardy said approvingly. He admired the way his sons handled difficult cases.

"Keep investigating on your side of the Atlantic," he said. "Sam will try to find out who peddled the stuff. I'll say good-by, but Aunt Gertrude wants to tell you something."

Gertrude Hardy, Fenton's sister, was a spinster with a sharp tongue. She frequently criticized the boys, but was secretly proud of them.

"I hear you're mixed up with witches," she sniffed. "Is that true?"

"It's true, Aunt Gertrude," Frank admitted.

"Well, be careful," she continued in a worried tone. "Just remember, witches often don't appear to be what they really are."

"We'll be careful," Joe promised. "Good-by, Aunty."

Frank hung up and they went to the departure gate where the Dublin flight would originate. Suddenly three men ran past. The sound of pistol shots rang out. Bullets whined through the airport!

CHAPTER XV

SOS in the Irish Sea

"HIT the deck!" Joe yelled.

He and Frank plunged headlong onto the airport floor. People ran helter-skelter. A number of policemen surged through the frightened crowd, captured the gunmen, and took them off.

"They're terrorists from abroad, shooting at each other," said a bobby. "But we got 'em all. Nobody's been hurt."

"Thank goodness those guys didn't kill anyone," Joe said. "Frank, isn't it a thrill to live in today's world?" he added sarcastically.

"Not that bad, Joe. How about centuries ago, when people were accused of riding broomsticks —and burned? I'm glad to be away from spooky Griffinmoor for a while."

They boarded their plane, which quickly became airborne. England vanished beneath their wings and they were over the Irish Sea. The plane bounced in the turbulence of air currents and down drafts. The stewardesses went down the aisle, calming the passengers.

"Pretty rough for an hour's flight," Frank grumbled.

"Any rougher and we'll end up in the drink," Joe agreed.

After landing at Dublin Airport, they caught a taxi to Tara Lodge. The driver took them down O'Connell Street, Dublin's broad main avenue, across the Liffey River, and out past Phoenix Park. Tara Lodge was situated in the middle of a lawn that looked like a great green carpet.

Colonel Melvin Stewart was a tall man with a mane of white hair. When he heard that the Hardys were friends of Professor Rowbotham's in Griffinmoor and working on his case, he gave them a warm welcome. He introduced his grandson Pat, a genial Irish youth of Joe's age, who was staying with the colonel for a few days.

The boys told him they were interested in Lord Craighead's disappearance and asked if he could give them any information.

"I'll be glad to tell you all I know," the old gentleman said, "but you'll have to wait a while. I have an appointment with my solicitor in half an hour."

Pat spoke. "Maybe you'd like to come with me in the meantime. I'm off to Phoenix Park for a game of rugby. We could use a couple of halfbacks. How about it? You Yanks know how to play rugby, don't you?"

The Hardys confessed they had played only once in an exhibition at Bayport High School. They would like to play again.

"Well then, off you go," the colonel said.

The three boys walked to the field house and joined the rest of the team. Uniforms were found for Frank and Joe. They all ran out onto the field and the game began.

The ball bounced crazily across the ground.

"Take it, Frank!" Pat bellowed.

Frank grabbed the ball, ran a few steps, and was tackled. He passed off to another player. The ball moved down the field. Pat got hold of it.

"Go for the goal!" Frank shouted.

Pat scored. Then the players gathered around the ball in a scrum. They kicked and shoved until Joe managed to work the ball loose. He turned sharply and suddenly slumped to the ground. Pat ran up.

"I say, are you hurt, Joe?"

"It's my trick knee. I twisted it in a football game at Bayport High."

Pat and Frank helped Joe to the sideline. Another player took his place and the game went on, with Pat scoring the winning goal.

Joe needed assistance to limp back to Tara Lodge, where Colonel Stewart inspected his knee.

"Painful but not dangerous," the old soldier

diagnosed. "Here, I'll tape it for you. Your knee will be as good as new if you stay off it a day or so."

He offered the Hardys the hospitality of his home, which they gratefully accepted.

After dinner, Pat put a couple of logs on the irons in the fireplace and built a roaring blaze. Colonel Stewart drew his chair close to the hearth and invited his guests to join him.

"So you want to know about Lord Craighead? It was just five years ago. I expected him to arrive here at Tara Lodge. When he failed to appear, I got in touch with Craighead Castle. Goodman said he had left Craighead, ostensibly on his way to Dublin. Apparently he vanished!"

An idea struck Frank. "Maybe he had an attack of amnesia. Lost his memory."

"Possibly," Stewart said. "When I knew him in the army, he often acted strangely. He was a loner, introspective—always seemed to be thinking about something he didn't care to divulge to anybody else."

Excitement gripped Joe. "Lord Craighead might have been hiding a mysterious secret!"

"That's also possible," his host replied. "But my guess at the time was that he was worried about financial problems."

"I've heard," Pat interjected, "that the castle is loaded with debts."

Frank looked doubtful. "I thought Lord Craighead was rich. Didn't he have zillions of pounds?"

Stewart shook his head. "The aristocracy is burdened by taxes. And it costs a fortune to run a castle. That's why so many people are selling. By the way, was the Craighead land sale ever completed?"

The question made the Hardys gape in total amazement.

"That's new to us, Colonel," Frank conceded. "Can you tell us about it?"

"I suppose it won't hurt to now. You see, Lord Craighead was trying to sell all his property to a London syndicate. One thing was holding the deal up. The syndicate demanded a package transaction, including the Craighead estate and Eagleton Green. But the craftsmen at the artisan village threw a spanner into the works. They refused to sell."

"So the deal fell through?" Frank asked.

"As far as I know." The colonel offered no more on the subject, and the session broke up.

In their room, the Hardys discussed the possibility that Milton Craighead was still attempting to arrange the land sale.

"Maybe the syndicate is trying to drive Eagleton Green out of business by means of sabotage," Frank speculated.

"And perhaps Matthew Hopkins has something to do with it," Joe said. "He's in real estate, remember? He could be connected with the same syndicate."

Joe spent the next day in Colonel Stewart's spacious walnut-paneled library, reading and resting his leg on a leather hassock. Frank and Pat, meanwhile, went to the Dublin Library to see what they could find about the genealogy of the Hardy family.

They ordered several enormous tomes at the desk, took them into the reading room, and leafed through the material. They spent an hour in hushed concentration.

"Lots of Hardys still in Ireland," Pat said.

"Sorry to say we lost track of the old timers," Frank confessed. "Look, here's a note. It seems our ancestors emigrated to America in 1800. Fenton is an old family name among the Hardys of Ireland. So that's where my father's first name comes from. He'll be interested to hear that."

"You chaps are a distinguished clan," Pat complimented him.

Frank returned the compliment. "Not so distinguished as the Stewarts. They used to be kings of England."

"It was a different branch of the family," Pat responded with a grin. "I can't claim succession to the throne!"

They deposited the volumes at the desk, left the library, and walked to a bus stop. Dublin was alive with crowds and traffic. Motorcycles whizzed past Trinity College, where the statues of Edmund Burke and Oliver Goldsmith stood. Men raised tankards and sang drinking songs in pubs. Pedestrians waited for the lights to change at the tall pillar on O'Connell Street.

Frank and Pat caught a bus to Phoenix Park and walked to Tara Lodge. Joe's knee was nearly back to normal. He told them he had been reading a book on witchcraft.

"It's about witches on the Isle of Man. There are two covens, one good and one bad. Good witches practice white magic. They're out to help humanity."

Frank chuckled. "I guess the black witches wear black hats."

"Well, they practice black magic," Joe said. "And specialize in curses. They stick pins in dolls and hex people."

Pat had been listening, amused at Joe's enthusiasm. "The Isle of Man is famous for its two covens," he said. "Also for the Hall of Magic, the museum. But why are you chaps so interested in witchcraft?"

"Ever since we started working on the professor's case in Griffinmoor we're plenty interested," Frank replied.

"And we were hoping to go to the Isle of Man, anyway," Joe explained, "to follow a clue." He told Pat about the striped cap they found at Stonehenge.

"There's a ferry that runs every day," Pat told them.

Frank nodded. "I think we should go tomorrow."

Colonel Stewart agreed when he heard about their plans. The next morning, Frank and Joe downed a stack of pancakes, thanked Colonel Stewart, and said good-by to Pat. A taxi took them to the dock, where they boarded the ferry for the Isle of Man.

Soon it edged away from the pier and headed downriver into the Irish Sea. Passengers lined the rails, facing a rising wind. The engines pulsated rhythmically as the vessel churned beyond sight of land.

Frank and Joe went into the lounge, where they ordered soda pop and sat down to talk over their situation.

"What do we do first?" Joe asked.

"Check out the cap. Then we'll try to find out as much as we can about the covens and visit the Hall of Magic."

They finished their drinks and went out on deck. The ferry was beginning to pitch and roll in stormy weather. Foaming waves broke over the bow. Sea spray swept across the deck and everybody on it.

The sky darkened as banks of clouds massed overhead. A bolt of lightning streaked toward the horizon and the wind rose to gale force.

"We're heading into an honest to goodness nor'easter," Frank predicted.

"Or whatever they call 'em in the Irish Sea," Joe added. "The crew had better batten down the hatches!"

As rain began to fall, crewmen appeared in boots and oilskins and prepared for the storm. They gathered deck chairs; then they coiled ropes and made sure the portholes were securely closed and bolted.

The Hardys moved toward the lounge with the other passengers when Joe gripped Frank's arm and pointed to the crest of an approaching wave.

"That monster's going to hit us, Frank!"

The wave came on, cresting higher by the second. It crashed into the ferry amidships. The vessel staggered under the impact of tons of water, and began listing to starboard.

"We've sprung a leak!" Frank shouted, but his voice was lost in the howling wind.

He and Joe hurried into the lounge. The other passengers were huddled together, many of them panic-stricken.

The crew hauled hoses to bail water from the hold, but it did no good. The ferry listed more sharply.

The voice of the captain came over the inter-

com. "Don life jackets!" He could be heard order-
ing his radioman: "Send an SOS!"

A couple of crewmen rushed into the lounge
and handed out life vests. After the Hardys
slipped into theirs, they went to the other passengers and helped those who had trouble putting
them on properly.

"Everybody to lifeboat stations!" boomed the
captain.

There was frantic pushing and elbowing as
frightened people scrambled to the deck. By this
time the list was so bad that the craft was in danger of capsizing.

"Lower the lifeboats!" the captain ordered.
"Abandon ship!"

CHAPTER XVI

A Coven Feud

THE lifeboats hit the waves. The first were filled with women and children. The men piled in next, while crewmen manned the oars. The boats filled up quickly.

"There's no room for us!" Joe yelled. "We'll have to take our chances in the water!"

The upper deck was awash when the captain ordered the last of the crew to follow him over the side. The Hardys leaped into the sea and swam away as fast as possible. They had to get clear of the ferry to avoid being dragged down by suction when the vessel sank.

Safely out of range, they watched the death of the stricken ferry. The bow went under and the stern rose high in the air. For a moment she stood on end and then plunged into the depths!

Frank and Joe bobbed up and down like a couple of corks. They knew they were too far from land to swim for it, and the lifeboats had drifted away in the storm.

Joe yelled out to Frank, "What'll we do now?"

"Wait to be picked up!" Frank shouted back. "The SOS must have got through!"

Gradually the storm died. The waves became calm, the rain stopped, and the sun came out. Some dots on the horizon grew larger. They were rescue boats answering the ferry's SOS, and they began picking up survivors.

The Hardys yelled and waved frantically until one of the boats noticed them. It curved in a wide arc and stopped in a mass of frothy foam churned up by its propellers. The two were hauled aboard.

Frank's teeth chattered. "Boy, are we glad to see you," he told one sailor.

"Yeah," Joe added. "We were getting cold out there!"

"You're obviously Americans," the seaman observed. "How do *you* happen to be swimming in the Irish Sea?"

Joe told him who they were and where they were from. He described how they went from East Anglia to Dublin and caught the ferry for the Isle of Man.

"That's interesting," the sailor said. Just then a call came for him from the engine room and he left.

"Joe! Zipper your lip, will you!" Frank rebuked his brother. "We're supposed to be on our way home, remember, and we don't want our whereabouts to get back to Griffinmoor!"

Joe looked embarrassed. "Sorry about that," he said and added wistfully, "Too bad we lost everything in our suitcases."

"Not everything. I salvaged this before we abandoned ship."

Frank reached into his pocket and drew out the striped cap they had found at Stonehenge.

"Good thinking," Joe complimented him. "At least we can check out this clue."

The rescue boat pulled into the dock at Douglas, the capital of the Isle of Man. Cold and stiff, the Hardys went ashore. The Red Cross put them up for the night. They took showers, had a meal, placed their money flat on a table to dry, and went to bed.

Their clothes were ready to wear again in the morning. They had breakfast, thanked their hosts, and strolled to the center of Douglas. Joe was wearing the striped cap.

The label in it read *Cooper's Clothes*. They found the store on the Douglas promenade. Joe handed the cap to the clerk, a young man with blond hair and blue eyes.

"Recognize this?" he inquired. "Can you tell who bought it?"

The clerk turned the cap over in his hands. He peered closely at the cloth and opened his mouth to answer, when the proprietor of the store cut him off.

"No identification is possible," the man said. "We sell thousands of such caps every year. Sorry we can't help you."

He strode over to a rack of raincoats and began putting on price tags.

"I guess that does it," Frank remarked.

Joe twirled the cap on one finger. "For sale—cheap!" He grinned.

As they turned to leave, the clerk nodded slightly as a signal. He raised his eyebrows and looked toward the door, indicating that the Hardys were to wait for him outside.

Frank and Joe left the shop and sat on a bench, looking at the scene on the beach across the promenade. Half an hour later the clerk emerged from the store and approached the bench.

"Follow me!" he whispered as he walked past. He continued for a couple of blocks, entered a pub, and sat down at a secluded table in one corner. Frank and Joe joined him.

"It's lunchtime," the clerk said. "So we can chat a little. My name is Harry Burke."

The Hardys introduced themselves. They noted that the pub was frequented by rough men who seemed ready for anything. Most were drinking at the bar. Several were tossing darts at a board.

After the waitress had brought three orders of

fish and chips, Burk leaned over and spoke in a low undertone.

"I know that cap," the clerk declared, "because it has a flaw in the cloth. And I remember who bought it."

"Who?" Frank prodded.

"A man from East Anglia. I recall the incident because he demanded a lower price. He was a tough bargainer."

"Do you know his——" Frank began.

Zing! A dart flew through the air, its sharp point penetrating the middle of the table. It stood upright with feathers quivering.

Startled, Frank wrenched the dart loose and hefted it in his hand.

"Is it a habit of the natives here to shoot toothpicks at strangers?" he asked tersely.

"That wasn't meant for you. It was aimed at me!" Harry said.

"Why?" Joe asked.

"Witchcraft! There's a feud going on. It's the black witches against the white witches to see who dominates the Isle of Man."

Joe was incredulous. "Harry, are you saying you're a witch?"

"Yes. I'm a white witch."

Joe scratched his head. "I've read about the black witches and the white witches. As I get it, the black witches practice black magic and the white witches, white magic."

"Black witches worship Satan," Burk said. "We white ones bow to Diana."

"The Greek goddess with the bow and arrow?" Frank asked.

"Yes, Diana, the Huntress," Burk told him. "That's what the ancient Greeks called her. We white witches believe Diana is a principle of good in the world."

"What do white witches do when they get together?" Joe wanted to know.

"We meet in places like Stonehenge when the moon is full. We chant invocations to Diana and dance in the moonlight."

"Sounds interesting," Frank said.

"That's not all," Burk explained. "The good we do comes from our knowledge of herbs, an old wisdom handed down from one witch to another. We gather the herbs in the forest in the dark of the moon and make medicines from them."

"Magic cocktails!" Joe quipped.

"Medicines!" Burk stressed. "Many people are being healed right now through witch lore. Black witches hate white witches for the good they do."

The clerk turned his head and glared at the group at the dartboard. They glared back at him.

"I know who threw the dart," he informed the Hardys. "He intended it as a warning not to speak to you. Just for that, I'm going to tell you who bought the cap. He's a black witch from Griffinmoor. He goes by the nickname of He Goat."

"What does he look like?" Frank pressed. "Is he young or old?"

"Older man. Short. That's all I know. Now, let's get out of here before something worse happens."

Frank and Joe proceeded to the promenade, discussing the meaning of what they had just heard.

"That gets Nip off the hook," Frank said. He didn't buy the cap. But who's He Goat?"

"One of the fellows we tangoed with at Stonehenge," Joe said. "And Nip could still have been the other guy."

"You're right. Nobody's off the hook. We just have a new suspect in addition to everyone else. This mystery is too much! We've never been involved with one like this!" Frank said, discouraged.

"Well, we know one thing. The fellow who tried to trap us at Stonehenge is from Griffinmoor. Most likely it's He Goat himself. But why did he buy the cap so far away from home?" Joe asked.

"This place is alive with witches," Frank reminded him. "Maybe he visited the coven on the Isle of Man one time and picked it up during his stay."

"Crazy," Joe said. "Between white witches and black witches I'm slowly going crazy!"

Frank chuckled. "If we hang around long

enough, either faction might try to convert us!"

"No way," Joe said. "The black faction at Griffinmoor definitely doesn't want us around. I just wonder why the Isle of Man group objected to Harry Burke talking to us. Unless they know who we are?"

Frank was thoughtful. "I'm beginning to wonder. "Maybe our cover is blown already and someone in Griffinmoor has warned the club here that we are coming?"

They bought toothbrushes and some clothes, then sat down on another bench. Behind them rose a row of hotels catering to the tourist trade. Traffic moved along the broad thoroughfare between them and the beach, where vacationers were lying in the sand, throwing beach balls or splashing in the water.

Adding to the activity, a platoon of motorcycles decorated in all the hues of the rainbow roared past. The leader wore a bright-red helmet and a black-leather jacket. Giving his machine the run, he zoomed in and out of traffic while his buddies zipped along behind him. The onlookers cheered.

Frank asked a pedestrian why there were so many colorful bikes.

"The International Tourist Trophy Races," the man informed him. "The best drivers in the world come here every year to compete. You might say it's the Isle of Man Grand Prix."

"Where's the race track?" Joe inquired.

"Covers most of the Isle of Man. Starts just outside Douglas, goes west across the island to Peel, then north to Ballaugh, east to Ramsey, and south to Douglas.

"Bad country roads, hills, dust, sheep—there are a lot of obstacles on the course. Well, I'm off to see the bikes!"

He walked away as a horse tram came slowly along, an open-air carriage riding on rails bisecting the promenade. A couple of cyclists were pedaling up behind it. They looked familiar, and Frank focused his eyes on them sharply.

"Hey, Joe! See those guys over there on the bikes? One looks just like Phil Cohen. If the other one was fatter, I'd say they were our pals Chet and Phil."

Just then the two cyclists came abreast of the Hardys. The dark-haired, wiry boy with the glasses looked at Frank and stopped.

"Chet!" he yelled. "Look who's here!"

CHAPTER XVII

A Happy Reunion

CHET Morton, a tall, strapping youth who was the Hardys' best friend, almost fell off his bicycle.

"I don't believe it!" he shouted. "What in the world are the famous Bayport detectives doing so far away from home?"

"Detecting, no doubt." Phil chuckled. "Okay, spill it. What are you working on in these parts of the globe?"

"Just sightseeing," Frank said.

"Sure. And we're just off to a walk in the woods," Chet quipped.

"I thought you were on a cycling tour of Ireland," Frank declared.

"We were," Phil replied, "but we decided to pop over here for the motorbike races."

Chet varoomed like a motor revving up. "Those guys zip around the back roads like crazy! I'd like to be in on it!"

Frank and Joe knew that Chet was usually up to his ears in a new hobby.

"Is it motorcycles this time?" Joe asked.

"That is just one of my interests," Chet answered with an airy wave of his hand. "My main concern on the Isle of Man is——"

'Cats!" Phil chuckled.

Joe looked quizzical. "Cats? We have scads of 'em in Bayport!"

Chet shook his head and looked pained. "Not Manx cats. The ones without tails that this island is famous for. I'd like to get one and ship it home."

"I think you should stick to cycling," Frank declared. "That's a great way to get rid of extra pounds."

Chet grinned and patted his belt line. "Terrific, isn't it? I'll be so trim when I get back that I might beat you out for halfback on the football team!"

Phil and Chet were staying at an inn, so the four decided to go there and compare notes about what they had been doing since their last meeting in Bayport.

The inn was a ramshackle building in an alley near Strand Street, the main shopping district of Douglas. They had to climb three flights of rickety stairs to reach the room.

"This is the best we could do," Phil said. "Douglas is buttoned up for the races."

The room held a couple of beds and chairs.

Chet produced four bottles of root beer and sat down on the window sill.

"We cycled all over Ireland," he boasted. "You guys should have been here. I could have given you some lessons."

He chugalugged his root beer and patted his stomach. The other three sipped theirs slowly. Finally Frank placed his bottle on the floor beside his chair.

"You should have been with us," he countered. "We could have used a couple of backstops when the going got rough."

Phil pursed his lips. "As I surmised, you and Joe are on another case."

"Right," Joe confessed. He described their sudden departure from Bayport after Professor Rowbotham asked their father to help solve the burglary at the Witch Museum. He mentioned their adventures in East Anglia, London, and Stonehenge.

"Hey, we'd like a piece of the action," Chet said. "Bring on the witches! But don't expect me to ride a broomstick!"

"You couldn't get airborne on a broomstick anyway, Chet." Joe needled him. "You'd need to lose another twenty pounds."

"Well, we'd like an assist," Frank said. "We haven't gotten too far with the witch case. He explained the problem of the Stonehenge cap and the black witch known as He Goat.

"Harry Burk says there's a feud between black and white witches on the Isle of Man," Frank concluded.

"I've got news for you," Phil revealed. "Chet and I have been to Black Magic Hall. It's owned by a couple of black witches!"

Frank became excited. "Is it a good exhibition? We were planning to go."

Chet shrugged. "It's okay. But we didn't see the Super Exhibit. We would have had to pay an extra pound."

A sound on the landing made the four sit up and listen intently. Footsteps stealthily approached the door and stopped. Joe crossed the room silently and pulled the door open. A slatternly woman almost fell against him before regaining her balance.

"I'm the landlady," she declared. "I was just about to knock. Four in a room means you pay twice as much."

"Then we want two extra cots," Phil said.

The landlady told them to take the cots from a hall closet. They paid her and she went back downstairs.

"Was she eavesdropping?" Chet wondered.

"She may become the next suspect," Frank replied. "What say we all go to Black Magic Hall and see the special exhibit?"

"Okay," Chet said, and they left the inn.

The museum was located in a rundown area of

Douglas. The man and woman who ran it were brother and sister, who admitted they were black witches.

"Why shouldn't we be?" the woman demanded defiantly. "Witches have rights, too!"

"Suppose," Frank replied, "you let us have tickets to the museum."

The man took their money and handed them the tickets. His eyes followed the boys as they went inside.

The regular exhibition was good. They looked over witch dolls, masks, bells, and candles. They stopped before a black table covered with velvet cloth on which lay a wand, a crystal ball, two daggers that pointed in opposite directions, an astrology chart, and a sprig of mistletoe.

"Interesting but not suspicious," Frank judged when they had circled the room. "I don't see any of Professor Rowbotham's things here."

An arrow directed them up a flight of narrow stairs to a door with a sign reading: SUPER EXHIBIT. They entered a small dark room and closed the door behind them. Dim lighting illuminated the items on display.

The first was a witch's cauldron.

Joe whispered, "Frank, that's from the Griffinmoor collection! I remember the illustration in the catalog. The dent in the side is a dead giveaway!"

"And here's a skull and crossbones exactly like

Professor Rowbotham's!" Frank murmured. "And this mask! And this dagger!"

The Hardys told their friends that the Super Exhibit appeared to be made up of stolen pieces from the Griffinmoor Witch Museum.

"We ought to make those crooks confess!" Chet said.

"No good," Frank countered. "They'd only deny everything."

"But we must do something!" Joe urged.

Phil thought for a moment. "How about visiting a witch's coven? We might find some more proof that way."

The Hardys agreed to try Phil's idea. The four laid their plans and descended to the ground floor, where the two witches were talking in guarded whispers in a corner. They fell silent when they saw the boys approaching.

"I have a secret to tell you," Frank said mysteriously.

"Oh, is that so?" the woman sniffed.

"Yes, you see we're apprentice witches ourselves."

"Where from?" the man snapped.

The unexpected question caught Frank off guard. As he fumbled for an answer, Chet came to his assistance.

"Bayport, U.S.A."

"Witchmaster?" the man snarled.

"Chief Collig!" Joe said quickly.

Frank, Phil, and Chet had a hard time keeping their faces straight. Chief Collig was the head of the Bayport Police Department!

"Never heard of him," the woman said. "But then, we never heard of Bayport, either."

"You can find it on the map of the United States," Joe assured her.

Frank intervened. "We'd like to visit a coven while we're on the Isle of Man. Can you set it up for us?"

The black witches exchanged glances. Then the sister nodded. "Maybe we can arrange it for you."

"It will cost you ten pounds each," the man added. "Come back at nine o'clock tomorrow night. We'll be waiting for you."

Strolling back through Douglas, the Hardys discussed the situation with their pals. Phil and Chet agreed that forty pounds was a lot of money to invest in their adventure. They decided to cut the sum in half.

Frank and Joe would pay twenty pounds to visit the coven. Phil and Chet would tag along as backups in case of trouble.

"It will be worth twenty pounds if we discover any clues," Frank pointed out.

"But now that we've found the stolen items from Griffinmoor," Phil said, "shouldn't we notify the police immediately?"

"Not yet," Joe replied. "We don't have proof.

It would be our word against theirs. The Douglas police wouldn't have any reason to believe us. We'll have to get in touch with Griffinmoor first."

Frank turned his head slightly and looked out of the corner of his eye. "Keep walking and don't look back," he said in an undertone. "We've got a tail behind us."

Following his directions, Joe, Phil, and Chet strolled nonchalantly along as if they hadn't a care in the world.

Phil also spoke in an undertone. "Do you recognize him, Frank?"

"I sure do. He's the guy who threw the dart at Harry Burk in the pub!"

They turned a corner. So did their shadow. He pretended to be looking in the shop windows.

Frank said, "We'll go to the inn as if nothing were happening. If he follows us, he may tip his hand."

There seemed to be nothing better to do. When they arrived, the landlady was inspecting a batch of receipts at the desk. She ignored them.

Frank peered covertly out the lobby window. "Our shadow's headed this way. He's coming in!"

"What'll we do now?" Chet asked.

"You three go up to the room," Frank said. "I'll stay on the second-floor landing and keep watch."

Scuffing their feet, the boys made a lot of noise as they climbed the three flights of stairs. Frank silently remained on the second-floor landing. Then he tiptoed down as far as he could and peered over the bannister into the lobby.

Their shadow came through the door and advanced to the desk. The landlady leaned toward him and he whispered something into her ear. Then, furtively, he hastened out.

The landlady picked up the telephone and dialed a number!

CHAPTER XVIII

Kidnapped!

FRANK strained to hear what the landlady was saying, but she spoke in a voice too low for him to understand.

When she hung up, Frank tiptoed up the stairs to their room. Silently he opened the door, slipped inside, and told the others what had happened.

"I don't know what we're up against now," he concluded. "But we're sitting ducks. Maybe two of us should stand guard while two sleep."

His companions agreed, and Phil and Joe took the first shift. But the night passed without incident.

In the morning they held a council of war to plan their strategy for the day.

"We don't have anything on tap until nine o'clock tonight," Phil observed. "What say we spend the day at the beach?"

"Great!" Chet said, and his eyebrows waggled. "Maybe we can meet some girls!"

"Take it easy, Romeo," said Joe.

After breakfast they strolled to a bath house near the promenade, donned swimming trunks, and ran into the deep water. They swam around like seals for half an hour. Then they went to the beach and sprawled on the sand beside some other bathers. They began to chat.

Phil lowered his voice and said, "Why are these people smiling at us?"

"I noticed that, too," Frank said. "Maybe they're just friendly."

A woman heard him. "I'll tell you why," she said. "It's because you're very brave boys!"

"What do you mean, ma'am?" Frank was puzzled.

"Aren't two of you the Hardy boys?"

"Yes, we are. I'm Frank. This is Joe."

"Well, then, you'd want to read this."

The woman handed Frank a newspaper. Phil, Chet, and Joe gathered around him and read over his shoulder.

The London paper described the sinking of the ferryboat. Frank and Joe Hardy were named as the two American passengers who did not abandon ship until just before she sank, and were picked up by a rescue boat.

The captain was quoted. "They were very courageous," he said, "to take their chances in the

Irish Sea instead of trying to climb aboard a crowded lifeboat."

"Wow!" Chet exclaimed. "A couple of heroes."

"˜ndeed they are," the woman said, as Frank returned the paper and thanked her.

But he looked unhappy. "No wonder our cover is blown," he muttered. 'Our enemies know where we are for sure."

"Sorry," Joe said sheepishly. "It's all my fault for talking too much."

"Nothing you can do about it now," Chet said. "You're big shots and you might as well enjoy it."

"Oh, I hope you do!" the voice came from a girl behind Joe.

Startled, he turned around to look at the speaker, a willowy blond with a big smile.

"I mean, I hope you enjoy your stay on Man," she said. "My name's Shirley Evans. I live here."

After introductions, Shirley asked Chet and Phil if they had been on the ferry boat too, and when she heard about their bicycle trip, she listened politely to their experiences for a few minutes.

But it was obvious that she had her eye on Joe. After a while, she directed all her attention to him. Joe did not mind at all. They chatted gaily for a while, then moved away from the others, discussing foreign politics of their respective countries.

Chet shook his head. "What do you know? Joe's

being swept off his feet right before our eyes!"

"Obviously he's in love," Phil added. "Just look at him. His face is one big grin!"

Frank chuckled. "Shirley's very pretty. I would be grinning too if she'd picked me."

Phil laughed. "Some talk for a hard-boiled detective! I thought you only had work on your mind!"

"There's a place and time for everything. Hey look, we're in again!"

Shirley had stood up and was addressing all the boys. "Why don't you come and have lunch at my house? It's just on the other side of the promenade. Mum and Dad would be glad to meet you."

"Gee, thanks," Joe said, and he sprang to his feet.

But the others were reluctant. "We want another dip. Join you later."

Shirley gave her address, took Joe's arm, and left. At home, she introduced her new American friend to her parents. Mrs. Evans, a charming woman with close-cut hair, was involved in social work. Mr. Evans, a tall, stout man, was a lawyer. They welcomed Joe, served lunch, and plied him with questions about himself.

"Frank and I have just been to Dublin," Joe revealed. "We visited Colonel Stewart at Tara Lodge."

"That's quite a coincidence," Evans said. "I served under Colonel Stewart in the Army."

"Then you may have known the Marquis of Craighead! The one who disappeared five years ago. We're trying to find out what happened to him."

"Sorry, I didn't know Lord Craighead," the lawyer said. "But I remember when he vanished. It caused quite a stir in military circles. All kinds of rumors were about. One even placed him here on the Isle of Man!"

"How was that, sir?"

"A serving girl who had once worked in the kitchen at Craighead Castle took the ferry from Liverpool to the Isle of Man. During the voyage she saw a ragged, unkempt man who looked like Lord Craighead. She couldn't be sure. I tried to find him without success."

A ring of the doorbell announced the arrival of Frank, Phil, and Chet. They, too, had lunch while Evans repeated what he had told Joe.

"I couldn't believe the ragged man really was Craighead," the lawyer went on. "He was an aristocrat, who always dressed well."

"He could have been disguising himself to fool everybody," Phil commented.

Evans admitted the possibility.

Frank changed the subject. "Have you lived here long, Mr. Evans?"

"All my life. I was born here. This house belonged to my grandfather."

"Then you must know about the feud between the black and the white witches."

Their host nodded. "I've heard about it."

"These black witches," Chet asked, "where do they hold their big powwow?"

Evans laughed. "You mean, where does the coven meet? I've been told it's in an ancient moldering castle on the west coast of the island. That's all I can tell you about black witchcraft. The white witches are something else. Their headquarters are at the Witches Mill in Castletown."

"That's on the southeast coast," Mrs. Evans explained. "I've been there. It's quite respectable."

Shirley giggled. "Respectable, Mother? How can witches be respectable?"

"Well, Shirley, the couple who run the Witches Mill told me the coven prayed for rain at their last meeting. I call that respectable. Our farmers need rain."

After a little more chatting, the boys thanked their hosts and got up to go. Shirley said to Joe, "Don't forget to write to me," and added archly, "it will foster international understanding." Her father chuckled.

"I'll write, scouts honor," Joe replied as he left.

On the way back, Joe took a lot of good-natured teasing from the others about his new girl friend, but in their room the talk became serious.

"If that guy the serving girl saw was Lord Craighead," Phil wondered, "what was he doing on the Isle of Man?"

"Who knows? Perhaps he's still here, alive and well," Frank speculated.

"Maybe He Goat came here to see Craighead!" Joe exclaimed.

Chet flexed his biceps. "I'm ready to butt heads with He Goat!"

When night fell they returned to Black Magic Hall. The street was empty. A single dim light shone behind the drawn shades of the witch museum. Frank paused on a corner.

"Let's synchronize watches," he suggested. "It's five to nine. Joe and I will go in and join the coven. If we don't come out in an hour, you fellows rush to the rescue."

"Understood," Phil said. "Meanwhile, I'll watch the front of the building."

"I'll patrol the back," Chet promised.

"Okay," Joe said, "here we go."

The woman opened the door of Black Magic Hall when Frank tapped on it. An old dusty grandfather's clock began to sound the hour of nine as they entered. The strokes boomed through the murky museum, setting up echoes in a long dark passageway leading to the rear of the building.

The sound made Frank uneasy. "That clock bothers me," he whispered to Joe while the woman was bolting the front door. "It's like the countdown to a funeral."

The man they had spoken to the day before suddenly strode out of the dark passageway and confronted them.

"Have you the money?" he demanded.

Frank and Joe each handed him ten pounds.

The witch counted the bills carefully before putting them in his coat pocket.

"Never fear, the black witches will take care of you," he said with a sinister smirk.

"You'll have to wear this," his sister hissed menacingly.

She deftly pulled a black velvet hood over Frank's head and drew the string tight under his chin. Her brother did the same to Joe. The Hardys were blindfolded before they knew it.

They joined hands at a command from the woman, who took Frank by the arm and led him down the dark passageway. Joe followed and the man came last, gripping Joe's shoulder with fingers like iron claws.

The rattle of a chain told the boys that a door was being opened. They were pushed out of Black Magic Hall to a car with its motor idling.

"Hey, wait a minute!" Frank protested. "Where are you taking us?"

"You want to visit our coven, don't you?" the man asked. "That's where we are going. Now get in the car!"

Frank felt his way into the back seat and Joe stumbled in beside him. Both were uneasy as the car roared off.

'I wonder if Chet saw us," Frank thought.

Chet had spotted them, but the car shot away before he could do a thing. Racing around the building, he told Phil that the Hardys had been kidnapped. They frantically looked for a taxi, but the street was deserted.

"What'll we do?" Chet wailed. "They're gone, and we have no idea where!"

The car bearing Frank and Joe raced through Douglas, barreling along the streets and taking curves at high speed. The boys could feel the change from asphalt to a dirt road, and they realized they were in the countryside.

The driver cursed savagely when he had to slow down for a flock of sheep. Circling behind them, he made the speedometer jump again.

Joe estimated that they had driven for an hour when they began to feel salty sea air. The wheels bounced and jounced over roads pitted with potholes. Finally the driver braked to a jolting stop.

A couple of powerful men dragged the Hardys out of the car. Again they were ordered to clasp hands. Again they were led forward, blindfolded by the velvet hoods.

They went down a sloping ramp, through an open doorway, and up a stone staircase. Joe stumbled on the top step and fell.

The boys were blindfolded.

"Get up!" a harsh voice growled. "Move on or it will be the worse for you!"

Frank started to protest that they could scarcely breathe, let alone move, but his words got lost in the folds of his hood.

Joe scrambled to his feet. The march went on. A flagstone corridor led to a broad curve followed by a sharp corner. There were more stairs and more corridors.

By now Frank and Joe were completely confused about the route.

"That's the idea," Joe thought. "They're taking us the long way so we won't know where we are."

Frank, who had been trying to memorize the many turns and twists of the route, gave up in despair. "A white mouse in a maze is a lot better off than we are," he said to himself. "At least the mouse can see!"

Rough hands brought the Hardys to a sudden halt.

"The moon is full," said a strange voice.

"The sun has set," responded the man who had growled at Joe on the staircase.

"Since you know the password," the strange voice continued, "only one question remains. Who are these two strangers?"

"Sacrifices!"

The word gave the boys cold chills.

"Are you sure of their identity?" the strange voice demanded.

"Yes. I followed them to their inn. The landlady gave me their names—Frank and Joe Hardy. She passed the information to Black Magic Hall. That is how we trapped them."

"Well done. You may pass."

The boys were pushed forward and hustled down one last flight of stone steps. They heard a key turn in a lock. A door screeched open and the two captives were hurled headlong into a room as cold and dank as a dungeon. A chatter of eerie voices greeted them. Then all was silent until a man spoke with a gloating cackle.

"He Goat, unmask them!"

CHAPTER XIX

The Torture Chamber

HE Goat's fingers loosened the drawstrings and whipped off the velvet hoods. Frank and Joe got to their feet and blinked.

They were horrified by the scene before them. They found themselves in a large stone chamber with no windows. Rows of black candles flickered from sockets in the walls. Blazing logs on a big hearth sent tongues of flame flicking up the chimney.

Ten men and women stood in a semicircle facing the boys. All wore hideous witch masks. He Goat was unmistakable, since his mask was the head of a goat with a protruding snout and short, curved horns.

A wooden throne stood against one wall, and upon it sat a man representing Satan. His ghastly mask was crowned by a weird headdress of purple and white feathers. He held a wand in one hand

and a sword in the other. At his elbow stood a crystal ball on a tripod.

The eyes of the evil creature glistened from the firelight as his gaze bored through the Hardys.

Now for the first time Frank and Joe noticed an open coffin lying at Satan's feet. In it was a body, but the boys were unable to get a clear view of the cadaver.

Finally Satan intoned, "There are now thirteen present. That makes a coven, assuming that our two apprentice witches are genuine."

Abruptly he leaned forward and waved his wand over the body of the coffin. His voice became hoarse as he croaked, "Abracadabra! Abracadabra! Abracadabra!"

The other witches took up the chant, which rose in a howling crescendo, making the Hardys' blood run cold.

Then Satan leaned back on his throne and mumbled an incantation. He pointed the sword at the boys and shook his feather headdress ominously.

"Do you wish to survive this encounter?" he snarled.

"Yes, we do," Frank answered.

"You must swear allegiance to me, Frank and Joe Hardy!"

Obviously this diabolical character knew them. But whose face was concealed behind that mask in the nightmarish charade?

The man spoke again. "You must swear allegiance to me!"

Joe clenched his fist and screwed up all his courage. "Nuts to you!" he replied.

"Second the motion!" Frank blurted out.

Satan shook with rage. "You cheeky impostors! You're no apprentices! No!"

His seething voice became a low whine. "You had your chance to leave England. We gave you plenty of warnings. You refused to heed. Now you will remain with us *forever!* He Goat, prepare the rack! But first, the potion!"

Several men seized the boys, pinioning their arms and forcing their heads back. Two women came forward with gold flagons in their hands. The metal gleamed in the dim light.

Frank recognized the crest—a griffin carrying off a knight in armor and the legend: *Avoir la Serre Bonne.*

The flagon was from Professor Rowbotham's Witch Museum! A split second later Frank felt something cold touch his lips. The witch tilted the flagon and a bitter liquid streamed into his mouth and down his throat. He choked on it.

Joe was also forced to swallow the fluid. They felt themselves growing faint.

"They've poisoned us!" Frank coughed.

Satan cackled. "It would be fortunate for you if we had. This potion will make you easier to handle, that is all. We want you to be awake for the climax."

"The climax?" Joe gasped.

"The rack!"

Two medieval torture instruments occupied one corner of the room. They looked like wooden bed frames with slats held together by thick ropes. But the head and foot of each frame were movable and could be extended by a winch.

The Hardys were thrown on the racks. Their hands and feet were bound tightly in a spread-eagle position.

He Goat chuckled. "Now we are going to give you the treatment!" As he turned toward the winch, his mask slipped far enough to reveal his face.

Goodman, the Craighead butler!

"How did you get here?" Frank cried out.

He Goat adjusted his mask and chuckled again. "It doesn't matter that you know who I am. You won't tell anybody."

Seizing the handle of the winch, he began to turn it. Frank felt his arms and legs drawn taut by the ropes. The stretching continued, causing sharp pains in his wrists and ankles.

Another witch turned the handle of the rack Joe had been tied to. The pain became agonizing, and when the boys cried out for help, the witches erupted into spasms of fiendish mirth.

They ceased at a signal from Satan. "That will do for now," he commanded. "The torture will resume in a moment. Keep the racks in readiness."

Descending from his wooden throne, Satan approached the Hardys. He drew a large, ornate key from under his robe and flaunted it in their faces.

"This is the key of death!" he cackled. "Look well at it!"

"What—is—it?" Joe gasped.

"The key to the door of your tomb!"

He was about to say something else when a small red light in the ceiling blinked on and off.

"Visitors!" Satan hissed. "To your work—all of you!" He handed the key to He Goat. "Keep this for me. I want to use it later."

Frank and Joe were released from the ropes that held them and hauled to their feet. The witches draped the black hoods over their heads and pushed them to an exit. Again a car with motor idling awaited them.

In the fresh air the boys became alert. They ripped their hoods off and sailed into the witches, who were attempting to force them into the car.

"Let 'em have it!" Frank shouted as he gave He Goat a karate chop.

"But good!" Joe exploded, hitting another witch with a haymaker.

The whole coven seemed to be there, except Satan. Witch robes were shredded and witch masks torn off as the Hardys battled their captors.

The fight was still raging when footsteps were heard pounding inside the building. The witches ran. He Goat jumped into the car and sped off.

"Are you all right, Joe?" It was Shirley's anxious voice.

"Yes—eh—fine. But you came just in time!" Gratefully the boys looked at their rescue squad —Chet and Phil, accompanied by Mr. Evans and his daughter.

Frank fought for breath as he gave Chet a weak slap on the back. "How'd you find us?"

Chet told him that he saw the Hardys taken out the back door of Black Magic Hall. "Phil and I had no way to follow you. So we went to Mr. Evans and asked him where the old castle was where the black witches met."

"I happened to know it was here," the lawyer told them.

"So, we drove over at once," Shirley added.

"We heard an alarm bell ringing in the castle," Phil said. "The witch sentinels must have spotted us. Anyway, we rushed the front door and ran through to the back."

Frank and Joe quickly explained what had happened after the kidnapping. Then they led the way into the castle and attempted to find the room in which the witches had held them captive.

They went up and down stairs and along the corridors of the decrepit building. They pushed doors open and cased room after room. Each was empty!

"We were blindfolded," Frank pointed out. "That's why we can't retrace the route."

"We made more turns than a ball in a pinball machine," Joe said.

They went back out to the spot where the fracas had occurred. Chet stubbed his toe on something lying in the grass. It was a large, ornate key!

"That's the one Satan waved at us!" Frank said. "He gave it to He Goat!"

"You mean Goodman," Joe observed. "He must have dropped it when you hit him with that karate chop."

"Maybe it fits one of the doors in this place," Phil said.

"Let's try it," Frank suggested, and the boys went back into the ancient castle, followed by the Evanses. But the key did not fit any of the doors.

"Perhaps it belongs to Craighead Castle," Joe said. "After all, Goodman lives there!"

"You're right!" Frank said excitedly. "We'll have to try it!"

"That can wait," Evans suggested. "We had better report to the police that strange things have been going on here. Come with me."

He drove to the nearest town and parked in front of police headquarters. They all took turns explaining to the sergeant on desk duty.

"So you see," Frank concluded, "the castle is being used by a coven of witches."

The sergeant shook his head. 'I doubt that we have the authority to do anything about it. Witch covens are not illegal."

"But they were torturing these boys!" Mr. Evans protested.

The sergeant raised his eyebrows. "That's different. We can't have that sort of thing going on. I'll round up some of my men and a police dog, and we'll give the place a thorough search."

Within minutes they were on their way back to the castle. The Evans car followed the police, and both vehicles drew to a stop in front of the building.

The sergeant took the police dog on a leash and held an abandoned witch mask under his nose. After sniffing, the animal padded around the castle and stopped at a grove of bushes. Behind the shrubbery was a sloping ramp.

"This is where we entered!" Frank exclaimed. "The dog's a better detective than we are!"

The animal went down the ramp, tugging at his leash, and up a flight of stairs.

"This is where I tripped!" Joe said.

The dog began moving around corners, along corridors, and up and down more stairs until he reached one last flight of steps going down. Whining eagerly, he stopped at a flush panel.

The sergeant pushed it. Nothing happened. Then he tried to slide it open. It moved!

"This is it!" the Hardys cried in unison.

They all entered the quiet dungeon and looked about. The candles were still flickering and the air was pungent with smoke from the dying fire. Satan's wood throne stood empty against the wall.

"There's the coffin!" Joe said. Shirley covered her face with her hands while the others stepped forward. Inside the box was the mummified body of a man whose wizened features were contorted into a savage scowl.

"John Pickenbaugh!" Joe gasped. "The witchmaster of East Anglia!"

All were appalled by the spectacle of the mummy. Even the police could not repress a shudder. The dog sat down, raised his muzzle toward the ceiling, and howled mournfully.

Something suddenly moved in the shadows behind Satan's throne. Shirley turned to look, then screamed out in terror!

CHAPTER XX

The Skeleton

IT was Satan himself! His repulsive mask looked more diabolical than ever in the flickering candle-light! The purple feathers of his headdress made him seem like a monstrous bird of prey!

Uttering an oath, he leaped from the shadows and flung himself on Joe. "I helped you!" Satan screamed. "And you ruined everything!"

The police overpowered him while he struggled, kicked, and shrieked. Frank ripped off the satanic mask and stood dumbfounded.

"Doctor Burelli!"

"My dentist!" Joe exclaimed. "So you're the new witchmaster of East Anglia!"

The Evanses looked on open-mouthed as the drama unfolded.

"That workshop in your basement gave you a great cover," Frank said. "We never guessed you were making masks for your witches as well as for your Gravesend Players!"

Joe's mind was working at top speed. "You're the one with the shock of gray hair and the bushy beard, Burelli. You carried the sword at John Pickenbaugh's funeral."

"And you had Pickenbaugh's body dug up afterwards and brought it here!" Frank went on. "But why?"

"It is a satanic relic!" Burelli screeched at them. "Do not touch it, ever!"

"Who'd want to?" Frank said. "And when we got interested in your satanic relic, you had us pushed into the open grave. And you had Ellerbee harrass us."

Burelli's smile was evil.

"He was probably He Goat's accomplice at Stonehenge," Joe said. "The 'friendly old man' who gave Professor Rowbotham the fake message and planted the cablegram."

"Now I get it!" Frank said. "Remember, Goodman has a cousin in New York? No doubt he sent it!"

"And it's obvious who robbed the museum in Griffinmoor," Joe deduced. "The purple feather fell out of the good doc's fancy Easter bonnet!"

Chet nodded. "He probably wore it to frighten anyone who might surprise him. And it sure would have worked!"

"Robbery, eh?" one of the policemen took up

the thread. "But why would a black witch rob a witch museum, of all places?"

By now Burelli realized he had lost. "We needed money for our coven," he said dejectedly. "And being black witches, it was easy for us to sell the artifacts as family heirlooms."

"Was Sears in on it?" Joe asked.

"No. He's innocent."

"And Milton Craighead?"

"He is too."

Frank nodded. "And when we tried to find a clue in the empty museum, someone familiar with the place turned off the master fuse. Was it you?"

"Yes. I wanted to scare you out of the building. All your snooping could come to no good."

"When we found the imprint in the cement and went to Lance McKnight for a cast," Joe said. "He sent us off to Hopkins and London into the hands of enemies. Black witches too, no doubt."

"McKnight? Hopkins?" Burelli looked surprised. "They're not witches. I had nothing to do with them."

"What about the key you waved at us before?" Frank pressed on.

Burelli's eyes narrowed. "You'll never find it!" he said craftily.

Frank drew it out of his pocket. "Here it is. Goodman dropped it!"

The dentist erupted into another paroxysm of

fury. "No!" he bellowed. "You can't have it! The key is mine! Do you hear? Mine!"

Since he refused to calm down, the police dragged him out of the castle and put him into the back seat of their car. It took two bobbies to hold him.

"We'll arrest him," the sergeant said. "And round up the rest of the black witches."

"By the way, the special exhibit at Black Magic Hall was stolen from Griffinmoor," Frank said, and he explained their mission to England.

"We'll see that everything is returned," the policeman promised, then got into the front seat. The dog leaped in beside him, and the car drove off.

The Hardys and their friends returned to Douglas. When they had said good-by to the Evanses and were back in their room at the inn, Frank said, "We'll go back to Griffinmoor as soon as possible and see if that key belongs to Craighead. Want to come?" he asked Phil and Chet.

"I'd rather stay for the motorcycle races," Phil said.

"And I want to corral me a pair of Manx cats," Chet added, "and go into business. They should be a hit in Bayport."

Next morning Frank and Joe flew to London and then went to Griffinmoor. They told Professor Rowbotham that they had found stolen items of his collection on Man and that they would be returned to him.

"With the pieces from London and those Sam Radley found in New York," Frank said, "you'll have most of your collection back now."

"Ah—ah, that's splendid," Rowbotham stated. "The Witch Museum can reopen. The case is solved, thanks to you."

"Not yet, professor," Joe told him. "The key we brought back from the Isle of Man has to be checked out."

"There is something you—ah—ought to know before proceeding," Rowbotham declared. "It is said that Eagleton Green will be sold to the London Syndicate. They will have a mass meeting this afternoon."

"Good. How would you like to be the star speaker?" Frank said. Rapidly he laid out their suspicions about the criminal pressure being put on the artisan colony to sell out.

"You can throw the wrench—er—spanner in the works," Joe said.

"I say," the professor replied, "that would be—ah—proper retribution. I'll do it!"

Frank and Joe, meanwhile, drove to Craighead Castle, accompanied by a constable with a search warrant. Joe brought a flashlight.

When Mrs. Goodman saw the Hardys, her eyes opened wide in disbelief. "You—you——"

"Yes. We returned in one piece," Frank said. "Where's your master?"

"And we don't mean witchmaster," Joe added.

The woman said Milton Craighead was in London. When she turned to hurry off the officer restrained her.

"I need you as a witness," he said. "I have a warrant to search this castle."

"Why?"

"To see if this key fits," Frank said, displaying the ancient relic.

Mrs. Goodman's hands began to tremble. She took a deep breath. "Where would you like to start?"

"In the turret," Joe said. "More specifically, in the armor room."

Shakily, the housekeeper led the way up the stone stairway and stopped before the storage room. The policeman opened the door, and Joe shone his light inside. Then all three searched amid the relics of medieval warfare.

Finally the constable said, "I say, what are we looking for?"

"A hidden door," Joe said. "Leading to a hidden room." He told of the outside window, located roughly in this area.

"Oh yes. I see. But there is no door in here."

"Hold it," Frank said. He stopped behind a suit of jet black armor. "Here's something." With both hands he pushed against a panel in the wall

It slid silently to one side, revealing an oak door about five feet high!

Frank pushed Burelli's key into the lock and exerted all his strength to turn it. Grating harshly, the lock snapped open.

The constable put his shoulder against the oak and pushed. The door swung back on creaking hinges. The trio ducked and entered a small chamber while the woman stood in the doorway.

It was musty with dust and cobwebs. Light came from the window Joe had noticed. It fell upon a treasure trove of witchery.

Charts bearing weird signs hung on the walls. Jars of herbs occupied the shelves. Cauldrons, wands, daggers, stuffed animals, and dolls pierced by pins were scattered around the room.

A ray of sunlight slanting through the window fell upon a bundle of old tweeds lying on the floor.

"Holy cow. Look!" Frank exclaimed.

From above the coat collar protruded a grinning skull! Bony hands extended from the cuffs!

The constable bent down on one knee to examine the label inside the jacket. On it was the name of a London tailor and the words, "Made exclusively for Lord Craighead."

"Good grief! We've found him!" Joe exclaimed.

Further scrutiny revealed that a vial was lying next to one hand, a piece of paper near the other.

Frank read it. "Looks like the formula for a potion," he said.

Suddenly the trio noticed that Mrs. Goodman had vanished. "I'll get her," the constable said. He hurried off, and in a few moments returned with the weeping housekeeper and Professor Rowbotham.

"I say, astounding news," the professor said breathlessly. "Lord—ah—Craighead. Really."

"Looks like it," Frank said and added, "I thought you went to the meeting."

"Most certainly. It's—ah—all over." He paused, looking down at the skeleton. "Poor fellow."

"How about this?" Frank said and handed him the paper.

"This is the formula for an ancient rejuvenation potion. It's in Lord Craighead's handwriting."

Frank shivered. "Then this must really be his skeleton! It's been locked in this room for five years!"

"Maybe he came in here to drink the potion and become young again," Joe theorized. "Perhaps it poisoned him."

The professor shook his head. "Only if someone exchanged the liquid in the bottle for another. The potion is harmless."

Rowbotham leafed through the papers on a small desk. "Here is more information," he said.

"It certifies that Lord Craighead was the witch-master of East Anglia! Dear me! And his assistant was John Pickenbaugh! They practiced the arts of witchcraft in this secret room!"

All the while Mrs. Goodman was watching with piercing eyes. Suddenly Joe realized where he had seen those eyes before.

"Mrs. Goodman," he accused her, "you're the palmist from the London witch collection. You were disguised when you stuck the needle into Frank's hand. The game is up. By now your husband has been arrested on the Isle of Man. He Goat is out of circulation along with the witch-master, Dr. Burelli!"

Joe's words struck the housekeeper like a thunderclap. She became hysterical, and finally confessed.

Pickenbaugh, she said, resented playing second fiddle to Craighead and poisoned him so he could be witchmaster. When he died, Burelli was next in line.

"And the doc didn't like us trying to find out what was going on here," Frank said.

"Yes, yes." the woman sobbed. Both she and her husband, at Burelli's order, had lain in wait in London. "He was disguised, too," she said. "We followed you to the underground."

"You also poured the oil on the castle steps, no doubt," Joe said. "And did you have Mary Ellerbee accuse us of malicious mischief?"

The woman hung her head.

"You'll have to come with me," the policeman said as he led Mrs. Goodman downstairs. First, he phoned the coroner, then the police station, with his report.

The boys and the professor, meanwhile returned to his home. Frank felt the usual letdown that came over him whenever they solved a case. Would there be a new adventure? He would have cheered up if he had known that soon they would be traveling to Zurich and Mexico in *The Jungle Pyramid*.

When they arrived at the professor's house, Sears served tea. He was shocked to hear that his sister was a witch.

"Her husband must have talked her into it," he said weakly. "Oh, it's terrible, just terrible!"

"Now tell us about the meeting," Joe said to Rowbotham. "What happened?"

"Everything is fine now. Ah—we caught the scoundrels!"

"For goodness sake, professor, give us the details. Who were the scoundrels?"

"The ones you suspected."

In what was virtually another interrogation, the Hardys pulled the story out of the professor. When he confronted Hopkins with the truth about his shady operation, the Londoner denied it all. But Nip Hadley came forward to confess his part in the arson plots.

"Said he did it under ah—duress," the professor said. "The law will go lightly with him."

"Then what?" Frank prodded.

Their host said that Hopkins and McKnight tried to sneak off. "They were about to drive away in McKnight's red MG when the infuriated artisans surrounded them."

"The red MG!" Joe exclaimed.

"Yes. Ah—I remember. It had the Motor Club emblem, as you once mentioned. There is now a charge against McKnight! By the way, he also admitted releasing his savage dog to frighten you after your visit to his shop."

"So Eagleton Green is saved," Frank said, grinning. "But, professor, there's still one thing that bothers us. What became of the poison?"

"What poison?"

"The stuff that was stolen from your museum. The jars of hemlock, aconite, and I don't know what all. We've got to find it before somebody else gets killed!"

Rowbotham held up a hand. "Ah—ah, there is no need to get excited."

"Why not?" Joe demanded.

"Because there is no poison. The jars were empty!"

Order Form
New revised editions of
THE BOBBSEY TWINS®

In *hardcover* at your local bookseller OR
simply mail in this handy order coupon and start your collection today!

Mail order form to: PUTNAM PUBLISHING GROUP/Mail Order Department
390 Murray Hill Parkway, East Rutherford, NJ 07073

ORDERED BY

Name _____

Address _____

City & State _____ Zip Code _____

Please send me the following Bobbsey Twins titles I've checked below.
All Books Priced @ $4.95

AVOID DELAYS   Please Print Order Form Clearly

☐ 1. Of Lakeport	448-09071-6	☐ 5. At Snow Lodge	448-09098-8
☐ 2. Adventure in the Country	448-09072-4	☐ 6. On a Houseboat	448-09099-6
☐ 3. Secret at the Seashore	448-09073-2	☐ 7. Mystery at Meadowbrook	448-09100-3
☐ 4. Mystery at School	448-09074-0	☐ 8. Big Adventure at Home	448-09134-8

Own the original exciting
BOBBSEY TWINS® ADVENTURE STORIES
still available:

☐ 13. Visit to the Great West   448-08013-3
☐ 14. And the Cedar Camp Mystery   448-08014-1

ALL ORDERS MUST BE PREPAID

_____ Payment Enclosed

_____ Visa

_____ Mastercard-Interbank #

Card # _____

Expiration Date _____

Signature _____
(Minimum Credit Card order of $10.00)

Postage and Handling Charges as follows

$2.00 for one book

$ .50 for each additional book thereafter

(Maximum charge of $4.95)

Merchandise total	_____
Shipping and Handling	_____
Applicable Sales Tax	_____
Total Amount
(U.S. currency only)	

Order Form

Own the original 58 action-packed
HARDY BOYS MYSTERY STORIES®

In *hardcover* at your local bookseller OR
simply mail in this handy order coupon and start your collection today!

Mail order form to: PUTNAM PUBLISHING GROUP/Mail Order Department
390 Murray Hill Parkway, East Rutherford, NJ 07073

ORDERED BY
Name _____

Address _____

City & State _____ Zip Code _____

Please send me the following Hardy Boys titles I've checked below
All Books Priced @ $4.95.

AVOID DELAYS   Please Print Order Form Clearly

☐ 1 Tower Treasure	448-08901-7	☐ 30. Wailing Siren Mystery	448-08930-0
☐ 2 House on the Cliff	448-08902-5	☐ 31. Secret of Wildcat Swamp	448-08931-9
☐ 3. Secret of the Old Mill	448-08903-3	☐ 32. Crisscross Shadow	448-08932-7
☐ 4. Missing Chums	448-08904-1	☐ 33. The Yellow Feather Mystery	448-08933-5
☐ 5. Hunting for Hidden Gold	448-08905-X	☐ 34. The Hooded Hawk Mystery	448-08934-3
☐ 6. Shore Road Mystery	448-08906-8	☐ 35. The Clue in the Embers	448-08935-1
☐ 7 Secret of the Caves	448-08907-6	☐ 36. The Secret of Pirates' Hill	448-08936-X
☐ 8. Mystery of Cabin Island	448-08908-4	☐ 37 Ghost at Skeleton Rock	448-08937-8
☐ 9 Great Airport Mystery	448-08909-2	☐ 38. Mystery at Devil's Paw	448-08938-6
☐ 10. What Happened at Midnight	448-08910-6	☐ 39. Mystery of the Chinese Junk	448-08939-4
☐ 11. While the Clock Ticked	448-08911-4	☐ 40. Mystery of the Desert Giant	448-08940-8
☐ 12. Footprints Under the Window	448-08912-2	☐ 41. Clue of the Screeching Owl	448-08941-6
☐ 13. Mark on the Door	448-08913-0	☐ 42. Viking Symbol Mystery	448-08942-4
☐ 14. Hidden Harbor Mystery	448-08914-9	☐ 43. Mystery of the Aztec Warrior	448-08943-2
☐ 15. Sinister Sign Post	448-08915-7	☐ 44. The Haunted Fort	448-08944-0
☐ 16. A Figure in Hiding	448-08916-5	☐ 45. Mystery of the Spiral Bridge	448-08945-9
☐ 17. Secret Warning	448-08917-3	☐ 46. Secret Agent on Flight 101	448-08946-7
☐ 18. Twisted Claw	448-08918-1	☐ 47. Mystery of the Whale Tattoo	448-08947-5
☐ 19. Disappearing Floor	448-08919-X	☐ 48. The Arctic Patrol Mystery	448-08948-3
☐ 20. Mystery of the Flying Express	448-08920-3	☐ 49. The Bombay Boomerang	448-08949-1
☐ 21. The Clue of the Broken Blade	448-08921-1	☐ 50. Danger on Vampire Trail	448-08950-5
☐ 22. The Flickering Torch Mystery	448-08922-X	☐ 51. The Masked Monkey	448-08951-3
☐ 23. Melted Coins	448-08923-8	☐ 52. The Shattered Helmet	448-08952-1
☐ 24. Short-Wave Mystery	448-08924-6	☐ 53. The Clue of the Hissing Serpent	448-08953-X
☐ 25. Secret Panel	448-08925-4	☐ 54. The Mysterious Caravan	448-08954-8
☐ 26. The Phantom Freighter	448-08926-2	☐ 55. The Witchmaster's Key	448-08955-6
☐ 27. Secret of Skull Mountain	448-08927-0	☐ 56. The Jungle Pyramid	448-08956-4
☐ 28. The Sign of the Crooked Arrow	448-08928-9	☐ 57. The Firebird Rocket	448-08957-2
☐ 29. The Secret of the Lost Tunnel	448-08929-7	☐ 58. The Sting of The Scorpion	448-08958-0

Also Available The Hardy Boys Detective Handbook 448-01990-6

ALL ORDERS MUST BE PREPAID

_____ Payment Enclosed

_____ Visa

_____ Mastercard-Interbank #

Card # _____

Expiration Date_____

Signature _____
(Minimum Credit Card order of $10.00)

Postage and Handling Charges as follows

$2.00 for one book

$ .50 for each additional book thereafter

(Maximum charge of $4.95)

Merchandise total   _____

Shipping and Handling   _____

Applicable Sales Tax   _____

Total Amount
(U.S. currency only)   [   ]

Nancy Drew® and The Hardy Boys® are trademarks of Simon & Schuster, Inc.,
and are registered in the United States Patent and Trademark Office

Please allow 4 to 6 weeks for delivery.

Order Form

Own the original 56 thrilling

NANCY DREW MYSTERY STORIES®

In *hardcover* at your local bookseller OR
simply mail in this handy order coupon and start your collection today!

Mail order form to   PUTNAM PUBLISHING GROUP/Mail Order Department
390 Murray Hill Parkway, East Rutherford, NJ 07073

ORDERED BY
Name _____

Address _____

City & State _____ Zip Code _____

Please send me the following Nancy Drew titles I've checked below
All Books Priced @ $4.95.

AVOID DELAYS   Please Print Order Form Clearly

☐	1	Secret of the Old Clock	448-09501-7	☐ 29	Mystery at the Ski Jump	448-09529-7
☐	2	Hidden Staircase	448-09502-5	☐ 30	Clue of the Velvet Mask	448-09530-0
☐	3	Bungalow Mystery	448-09503-3	☐ 31	Ringmaster's Secret	448-09531-9
☐	4	Mystery at Lilac Inn	448-09504-1	☐ 32	Scarlet Slipper Mystery	448-09532-7
☐	5	Secret of Shadow Ranch	448-09505-X	☐ 33	Witch Tree Symbol	448-09533-5
☐	6	Secret of Red Gate Farm	448-09506-8	☐ 34	Hidden Window Mystery	448-09534-3
☐	7	Clue in the Diary	448-09507-6	☐ 35	Haunted Showboat	448-09535-1
☐	8	Nancy's Mysterious Letter	448-09508-4	☐ 36	Secret of the Golden Pavilion	448-09536-X
☐	9	The Sign of the Twisted Candles	448-09509-2	☐ 37	Clue in the Old Stagecoach	448-09537-8
☐	10	Password to Larkspur Lane	448-09510-6	☐ 38	Mystery of the Fire Dragon	448-09538-6
☐	11	Clue of the Broken Locket	448-09511-4	☐ 39	Clue of the Dancing Puppet	448-09539-4
☐	12	The Message in the Hollow Oak	448-09512-2	☐ 40	Moonstone Castle Mystery	448-09540-8
☐	13	Mystery of the Ivory Charm	448-09513-0	☐ 41	Clue of the Whistling Bagpipes	448-09541-6
☐	14	The Whispering Statue	448-09514-9	☐ 42	Phantom of Pine Hill	448-09542-4
☐	15	Haunted Bridge	448-09515-7	☐ 43	Mystery of the 99 Steps	448-09543-2
☐	16	Clue of the Tapping Heels	448-09516-5	☐ 44	Clue in the Crossword Cipher	448-09544-0
☐	17	Mystery of the Brass-Bound Trunk	448-09517-3	☐ 45	Spider Sapphire Mystery	448-09545-9
☐	18	Mystery at Moss-Covered Mansion	448-09518-1	☐ 46	The Invisible Intruder	448-09546-7
☐	19	Quest of the Missing Map	448-09519-X	☐ 47	The Mysterious Mannequin	448-09547-5
☐	20	Clue in the Jewel Box	448-09520-3	☐ 48	The Crooked Banister	448-09548-3
☐	21	The Secret in the Old Attic	448-09521-1	☐ 49	The Secret of Mirror Bay	448-09549-1
☐	22	Clue in the Crumbling Wall	448-09522-X	☐ 50	The Double Jinx Mystery	448-09550-5
☐	23	Mystery of the Tolling Bell	448-09523-8	☐ 51	Mystery of the Glowing Eye	448-09551-3
☐	24	Clue in the Old Album	448-09524-6	☐ 52	The Secret of the Forgotten City	448-09552-1
☐	25	Ghost of Blackwood Hall	448-09525-4	☐ 53	The Sky Phantom	448-09553-X
☐	26	Clue of the Leaning Chimney	448-09526-2	☐ 54	The Strange Message in the Parchment	448-09554-8
☐	27	Secret of the Wooden Lady	448-09527-0	☐ 55	Mystery of Crocodile Island	448-09555-6
☐	28	The Clue of the Black Keys	448-09528-9	☐ 56	The Thirteenth Pearl	448-09556-4

ALL ORDERS MUST BE PREPAID

_____ Payment Enclosed

_____ Visa

_____ Mastercard-Interbank #

Card # _____

Expiration Date_____

Signature_____
(Minimum Credit Card order of $10.00)

Postage and Handling Charges as follows

$2.00 for one book

$ .50 for each additional book thereafter

(Maximum charge of $4.95)

Merchandise total	_____
Shipping and Handling	_____
Applicable Sales Tax	_____
Total Amount *(U.S. currency only)*	

Nancy Drew® and The Hardy Boys® are trademarks of Simon & Schuster, Inc.,
and are registered in the United States Patent and Trademark Office

Please allow 4 to 6 weeks for delivery